The Perpetual Book Fund

A
~~Donald A. Collard~~
Perpetual Book Fund Book

FRIENDS
Williamsburg Regional Library
FOUNDATION

D1575490

THE SECRET STARLING

JUDITH EAGLE

illustrated by JO RIOUX

WALKER BOOKS

Text copyright © 2019 by Judith Eagle
Illustrations copyright © 2021 by Jo Rioux

First US edition 2021
First published by Faber & Faber Limited (UK) 2019

Library of Congress Catalog Card Number pending
ISBN 978-1-5362-1365-2

21 22 23 24 25 26 LBM 10 9 8 7 6 5 4 3 2 1

Printed in Melrose Park, IL, USA

This book was typeset in Warnock Pro.
The illustrations were done in pencils and ink and rendered digitally.

Walker Books US
a division of
Candlewick Press
99 Dover Street
Somerville, Massachusetts 02144

www.walkerbooksus.com

A JUNIOR LIBRARY GUILD SELECTION

TO MR. MARKS

AND ALL THE TEACHERS WHO ENCOURAGE US

TO BELIEVE IN OURSELVES

JE

ONE

MOST PEOPLE BELIEVE A LITTLE ROUTINE IS A GOOD thing. Babies thrive on a routine of milk, cuddle, sleep; milk, cuddle, sleep; milk, cuddle, sleep. Schools tend toward a shipshape routine of lining up, lessons, and play. A good routine, say certain people, gives you a sense of purpose and adds structure and order to the day.

But the routine that Clara had to follow at Braithwaite Manor would send those very people half mad. Day in, day out, it was always the same.

Get up, wash up (in the freezing bathroom, where icicles hung in winter), have breakfast alone in the drafty dining room. The dining room, as always, would be deadly quiet except for the solemn tick of the grandfather clock and Clara's chewing noises, which seemed extraordinarily loud.

After breakfast came lessons, taught by a governess. The governesses changed almost on a monthly basis. "It's like life *ground* to a halt in the nineteenth century!" the last one had cried, grabbing her bag and click-clacking furiously down the hall to the door.

Clara couldn't agree more.

The house did, after all, look like something out of a Victorian gothic novel, crouching in the middle of the moors like an angry crow. A single dark turret rose up to stab the gloomy skies, and flinty little windows glittered meanly at anyone with the gumption to approach.

The governesses had strict orders from Clara's uncle to teach her the most boring lessons known to man or woman. Clara knew full well they would have preferred to do fun projects, like making collages, putting on shows, and writing stories. But Uncle didn't have a fun bone in his body and preferred the traditional approach: endless times tables, fiendishly hard spelling tests, and complicated grammatical exercises that made both Clara's and the governesses' brains hurt.

After lessons came lunch, and after lunch it was time for a walk in the scrubby grounds.

Perhaps if the sun ever shone, the garden might have held a bit more promise. After all, as certain grown-ups will tell you, there are endless games to be played in the great outdoors.

But at Braithwaite Manor, the sun rarely shone. Instead, the freezing wind whipped and whirled, and the rain spliced the air and grazed your face until it hurt.

So while the governesses swaddled themselves in fur coats found in the upstairs wardrobes and huddled on the bench reading old copies of *Vogue*, Clara hung around and kicked her heels on the half-frozen ground. She never felt like playing with the moldy old dirt and stones on her own.

After the walk came the dreariest part of all, the daily visit to Uncle. And here is the truth of it: Uncle was a cold man. Not a glimmer of warmth emanated from this sternest of beings. It is entirely possible that he had no real feelings at all. His eyes never twinkled. He rarely smiled. He didn't hug, or laugh, or cry, or do any of the things that warmer-blooded humans do. As far as Clara could see, the only things he liked were rules and routine.

"Children should be seen and not heard" was his favorite saying. Clara was not to run in the house, but must always tiptoe quietly. He detested chatter, so Cook and Clara had to wait until he went out, which was rare. There was no television or radio, and he did not get a newspaper. For all intents and purposes, they were quite adrift from the outside world.

Clara had wasted hour upon hour wondering why Uncle was so mean-spirited. One likely explanation was that he was permanently grief stricken. His parents had died suddenly when he was a very young man. His sister, Clara's mother, had died in childbirth, and Uncle had long ago made it clear that not one of the deceased was to be spoken about or referred to in any way. Clara knew she had a father *somewhere* out there in the great wide world, but she had stopped asking about him long ago.

"He doesn't even know you exist," Uncle had told her meanly. "How many times do I have to tell you before it gets into that woolly head of yours?"

The daily visits to Uncle followed a familiar pattern. There he would sit, deep in his armchair, in his cozy study in front of the one roaring fire, and gaze at Clara as though he wished she weren't there. Sometimes he would close his eyes, breathe deeply, and open them again in a kind of despair. It was at times like these that Clara couldn't help wondering if he would just prefer her to disappear.

Then he would ask the questions. The same questions he asked every day.

"How were your lessons today? What did you learn? Did you say your prayers?"

Clara barely heard the questions now, so familiar was

she with the mind-numbing tedium of it all. Anyhow, her answers were always the same.

"Good, Uncle," "Many things, Uncle," and "Yes."

The yes was a lie because Clara couldn't always be bothered to pray, just like she couldn't always be bothered to brush her teeth. Instead, she put her hands together, shut her eyes, and counted backward from ten.

Clara knew that if she changed her answers Uncle wouldn't bat an eye. Once she had tried it just to see. She'd answered, "Boring," "Nothing at all," and "I never do."

Then she'd squeezed her eyes shut and held her breath, waiting for Uncle to explode. Or at least to look at her and take notice. He did neither. It gave Clara a weird sinking feeling. At least now she was one hundred percent sure he didn't listen to her any more than she cared to listen to him.

After the visit to Uncle, it was supper time.

"What's for supper?" Clara would ask in the vain hope that Cook might say something interesting like coq au vin or beef Wellington or shrimp cocktail, some of the recipes she had read about in her governesses' magazines. But Uncle was a firm believer in plain meals—nothing fancy was allowed.

Recently the answer was always "spreadables": three slices of bread and margarine and a variety of jars on the table. The jars were full of untempting things like fish paste, strangely crunchy honey, and gloopy jam.

"Sorry," said Cook when Clara's face fell again. It wasn't Cook's fault. Clara knew that Uncle was terribly stingy with the housekeeping money. Last month he had halved Cook's budget, and two weeks later he had halved it again. Cook whispered to Clara that she was almost at her wits' end.

When supper was finished, it was time for bed. And that was it: the exact same thing, over and over, day in, day out, forever and ever, amen.

It was true that, occasionally, Uncle did disappear for a day or two. Then Clara, the governess of the month, and James, the butler, would join Cook in the kitchen for hot buttered toast and card games. If Clara was lucky, James would teach her some DIY skills. Now she knew how to saw wood, drill holes, and hammer in nails.

In bed, Clara would read until she couldn't keep her eyes open. Besides a scrap of red ribbon tucked inside her shell box, books were the only things she had of her mother's: a battered collection of paperbacks with yellowing pages, the flyleaf of each inscribed in violet ink:

PROPERTY OF CHRISTOBEL STARLING.
RETURN IF FOUND.

Clara loved to hold the open books to her nose, inhaling the musty oldness. Her favorite was *The Secret Garden*, which she had read again and again. It was a shame there was nothing remotely resembling a secret garden at Braithwaite Manor. Just a patch of scrub, a tumbling-down stone wall, and beyond that, miles and miles of desolate moor.

It was hard not to feel hopeless. But Clara tried her best to look on the bright side even though the days dragged interminably and there was no one to play with, nothing new to see.

TWO

DESPITE THE DEATHLY DULL ROUTINE, THERE WAS one thing at Braithwaite Manor that *was* changing. And that was the state of the house, which was slowly falling into terrible disrepair. Doors didn't close properly; windows creaked and gaped. Only last month a crack had appeared in a pipe in the governess's bathroom. Within weeks it had turned from a crack to a jagged fissure, and water, at first just a trickle, was now almost gushing out in a steady stream. James said there was nothing to do but put a bucket underneath to catch the drips. Soon one bucket became two, then three. The buckets needed emptying and replacing at all hours. No wonder James had dark circles under his eyes.

At the same time, Clara had started to notice things

disappearing. The first was the portrait of Uncle's ancestors in the hall. Clara wasn't sorry to see it go. It was a dark, gloomy painting, and she hated the way the ancestors always looked at her disapprovingly as she came down the stairs. It was almost as if they were agreeing with Uncle that she wasn't worth much.

Next to disappear was the huge blue-and-white china soup tureen decorated with dancing maidens that sat on the sideboard in the dining room. Many times Clara had asked Cook why they couldn't serve actual soup in it. But Cook always said the same thing: "It's an heirloom, ducks, and it's just for show."

Soon it was one thing after another. The bowl of silver eggs from the mantelpiece in the drawing room; an entire shelf of leather-bound books from the library; the series of small animal paintings placed at equal intervals up the stairs.

"Where's everything going?" Clara asked Cook. She missed the pictures of the foxes and farmyard animals. Now all that remained were ghostly white rectangles, the wall around them almost black from years and years of accumulated dust. But Cook just shook her head mysteriously and muttered something about "needs must."

Then the unheard of happened. The routine faltered.

Well, not just faltered—it ground to a halt. A week ago, the latest governess had left in a huff, loudly declaring that Uncle should be arrested for child cruelty. It wasn't the first time Clara had heard such words. Cook occasionally murmured them under her breath while casting sorrowful looks in Clara's direction. Clara wondered if it was true and decided not. She wasn't kept locked in an attic, or starved, or anything like that.

For five days, Clara was left on her own.

No governess meant no lessons, no walk in the garden, and no one reminding her to visit Uncle in his study before supper. Clara didn't complain or seek out Uncle to ask what was going on. Instead, she did the sensible thing: stayed quiet and kept out of the way. She invented her own routine, which was much nicer. Each morning she would slip into the library, silently do ten star jumps to warm up because it was like the North Pole in there, and then choose a book. On Monday she reread *The Secret Garden*; on Tuesday, *Thursday's Child*; on Wednesday, *Oliver Twist*; on Thursday, *Anne of Green Gables*; and on Friday, *Ballet Shoes*. Clara was especially fond of stories about children who were all alone in the world.

After that she followed James about. She liked to watch the butler quietly appraise the latest damage to the house, select the correct tools for the job, and tackle the repairs. Best of all was when she was allowed to help. Her favorite thing was to mix up the plaster until it looked like thick white icing and then fill the spidery cracks that lined the walls.

Later Clara would make her way to Cook's quarters. Uncle didn't like her in this part of the house in case she and Cook got chatting and disturbed the peace. But all week the study door stayed firmly shut, which meant Cook was quite free to regale Clara with tales about her family. Her son was married to Celeste, a nurse who had come all the way from the Caribbean; her daughter, Babs, was a dancer on a cruise ship and had traveled all over the world. There were heaps of grandchildren, all of whom seemed to have special talents. One of them could play "Chopsticks" on the piano blindfolded; another could do backflips and walk on his hands; the littlest one could touch her nose with her big toe.

The stories filled Clara with a strange yearning. More than anything, she would have liked to belong to such an interesting-sounding family as Cook's.

∽

On Saturday, the sixth governess-less morning, Clara woke, hardly daring to believe it would be another routine-free day. As usual, and because old habits die hard, she rose at seven, washed, shivered, dressed, and descended to the drafty dining room. It seemed draftier than ever, if that were possible. But what was really odd was the table. It hadn't even been set. How incredibly vast it looked when it was not set for one.

Even more strange, the table hadn't been polished. In fact, it looked like it hadn't been polished all week. Usually Clara could see her reflection in it. Now she wrote her name, with a swirl, in the dust.

Clara sat for a while and listened to the clock. No toast. No marmalade. Was the routine, Clara thought, utterly and actually dead?

And then, from the direction of the kitchen came the sound of sobbing. Was it Cook? Surely not. Quickly, Clara rose and hurried out of the dining room to Cook's quarters. Pushing open the green baize door, she breathed in deeply. She would eat her toast in here. It was warm and smelled of apples. But no. Here was Cook, slumped over the scrubbed pine table, her head in her hands. The sobbing noises *were* coming from her.

"Are you all right?" Clara asked anxiously. She had never seen an adult crying before.

"No, I'm not, ducks," said Cook, sniffing and raising a

tearstained face. "He's sacked me. Run out of money, he says, none to spare for wages, would you believe. I should have seen it coming, what with the measly housekeeping, not to mention the funny business with the family heirlooms."

"Oh," said Clara. She felt a nervous fluttering start up in her chest. Cook couldn't leave!

"Right," said Cook. "Come with me."

Clara followed Cook into the pantry. She wanted to grip her arm and plead with her to stay, but she couldn't because Uncle would accuse her of making a scene. Together they surveyed the almost-bare shelves. There were three dozen eggs, half a sack of potatoes, and a handful of vegetables so old they were starting to sprout hair and eyes.

"Not much, is there?" said Cook.

"No," agreed Clara, who knew next to nothing about supplies and how long they were supposed to last. All the same, she understood that no money meant no more food. "Not much at all."

"When you're hungry," said Cook, "take an egg and boil it in a pan of water. Five minutes if you want it soft, eight for hard."

"OK," said Clara, hoping she would be able to remember. Five for soft, eight for hard.

"Potatoes," said Cook, nodding at the sack. "Peel them if

you can be bothered, but don't worry if you can't. Boil 'em for a good twenty minutes. Mash them if you like."

Clara gulped. She had not expected a cooking lesson this morning. Was Uncle expecting her to cook for both of them? It was all rather a lot to take in.

Now Cook bustled back into the kitchen. Clara saw she was gathering her bags.

"Where's James?" asked Clara tentatively. Come to think of it, she hadn't seen the butler since yesterday morning.

"Already gone," said Cook, giving Clara a short, fierce hug. "Too upset to say goodbye." Clara felt a great big sob well up inside her, but she pushed it back down. Years of being the niece of a coldhearted uncle had toughened her up. She *wanted* to fling herself at Cook and not let go, but she told herself not to. Cook had her own children and grandchildren to look after. She could hardly go worrying about other people's children, even if there was a bit of child cruelty going on.

"Just you and Mr. S. now, dearie, but you're a strong 'un. You'll survive."

Clara drew herself up. If Cook thought she was strong, then she would be. Bold and fearless, like a heroine in a book.

"I won't be far," said Cook, taking a shiny new fifty-pence

coin out of her purse and pressing it into Clara's hand. Clara tried to give it back. It didn't seem right to accept money from someone who had just lost her job. But Cook said "Take it" in a funny, gruff sort of way, and then, "I'll be in the village if you need me."

Was that a tear in the corner of Cook's eye? Clara couldn't be sure, but she was inclined to think it was. Now Cook was turning to go. "Goodness knows I won't be able to find more work at my age."

THREE

THE VERY SAME DAY THAT COOK LEFT, UNCLE called Clara to his study.

"Clara!" he shouted irritably from the foot of the stairs. "Get down here now!"

This is odd, thought Clara, who was curled up on the window seat at the end of the third-floor corridor. It was highly unusual for Uncle to issue a summons outside of normal visiting hours. And it was especially unusual for him to break his "no shouting across the house" rule. But odd things had become a common occurrence in recent days.

As she glided into the study ("quiet, not clattering") Clara noticed that Uncle was not, for once, sunk deep in his chair. Instead, he was standing, twitching almost, and then he began pacing back and forth in a manner she had not observed before. Could he be ... *flustered*?

Whatever it was, it wasn't very Uncle-like.

"Clara," he began, pausing in a way that made Clara feel duty-bound to fill the silence.

"Yes, Uncle?" His study looked even more like a bomb site than usual. There were papers everywhere: teetering in skyscrapers, exploding in piles on the desk, anchored under books, tucked behind the pictures on the walls, scattered willy-nilly across the floor.

"Mind that!" Uncle barked as Clara almost tripped over a bundle of letters. *If he'd only tidy up it would make things a lot easier,* Clara thought resentfully. In the past, he had occasionally let Cook in to clean and keep order. But recently the study had been out of bounds to her as well.

The fire was unlit. He probably didn't know *how* to light it. That had been James's job. Clara had often watched the butler carefully sweeping the grate so that the ashes didn't turn to dust and billow into the air, layering up kindling and coal; sometimes he allowed Clara to strike the first match. Clara shivered and curled her toes inside her shoes.

"We are leaving," said Uncle abruptly, drumming his fingers on the mantelpiece, "before lunch. Pack a suitcase of indispensables and meet me in the hall in an hour."

Clara swallowed. Was there to be no explanation? "Uncle—" she began.

"Enough!" he snapped. "It's very important we leave on the hour." He nodded his head toward the door, which Clara knew very well was his way of saying "Get lost."

Clara trudged back up the stairs. A suitcase of indispensables! What on earth was that? And now that Cook had gone, she couldn't ask.

For as long as she could remember, an empty leather suitcase had sat on top of her wardrobe. She had never had a reason to use it before because she had never traveled anywhere. Now she stood on a chair and dragged it down.

What would a normal person pack if they were going away? Clara knew she wasn't normal from her books. She had never been to school, or to the sea, or swung on a swing in a park, or had pocket money to spend on chips or sweets or comics.

Occasionally she had made the half-hour walk across the moors with Cook to the village shop. Sometimes the shopkeeper gave her a jawbreaker so big it took almost the whole journey back to lick it before she could even fit it into her mouth. Twice a year she went with James in the ancient silver Mercedes to the shop in Leeds, where he stood twisting his cap while the assistants measured her and fitted her with new shoes. Clara loved those days and longed to linger, but Uncle always insisted they come straight back. Even so, on the return journey, James would park up in the village and they'd go into the café to shovel down tea and cake. It was always utterly marvelous.

Now what was going to happen? Where was Uncle taking her? Clara looked at her reflection in the mirror and saw a sharp, pointy face gazing expectantly back at her. Taking a length of hair, she combed it backward, the way she had seen her governesses do. She combed and combed until the cloud of blue-black hair looked like a bird's nest. Then she twisted it into a stately pile on top of her head. Turning this way and that, she admired her handiwork. The new hairstyle looked rather regal. *Now* she would be ready for anything.

Clara thrust a few items of clothing into the suitcase and filled the remaining space with books. Carefully, she tucked her shell box with the red ribbon into the corner. Then she zipped up the suitcase, negotiating the part where the teeth were crooked, buckled it tightly, and staggered downstairs.

∾

It wasn't until they were in the Mercedes, with Braithwaite Manor behind them and the bleak moor stretching out endlessly ahead, that Uncle spoke.

"I'll drop you in the village. I've got a couple of errands

to do. You know where Cook lives if you need anything."

What did he mean? What errands did he have to do? How long would he be? Clara opened her mouth and then shut it again. Somehow Uncle's expression didn't invite interrogation. His brow was furrowed and he stared straight ahead, his elegant hands wrapped around the wheel. He was dressed in his usual gray suit with the wine-colored waistcoat, a spotted silk scarf tied loosely at his throat. His thick dark hair was swept back from his high forehead. He would be quite distinguished-looking, Clara thought, if it weren't for the scowl.

A little glimmer of hope flickered at the furthermost reaches of Clara's mind. She was, after all, an eternal optimist. Perhaps Uncle was going to try to be a *better* uncle.

"Uncle," she blurted out, "where are we going?"

Now Uncle did look at her. Just a quick glance. They were approaching the village. A kind of deafening silence filled the air. Clara really thought she might burst.

"Never you mind," he eventually barked, and made a swatting movement with his hand, as if batting away a particularly annoying fly.

Clara stared out at the road. Her eyes burned. She hated him. Hated him! She wasn't going to ask him anything else, ever. She was never going to speak to him again.

FOUR

WHEN THEY REACHED THE VILLAGE, UNCLE stopped the car.

"Out you get, then," he said brusquely.

Clara wondered how long he was going to be, but she refused to break her silence. She was good at being stubborn. Uncle was already out of the car anyway, retrieving her suitcase from the trunk.

"Here," he said, thrusting it at her. It banged against her knee, sending little darts of pain up her leg. But before she even had time to wince, the door slammed shut and the car roared away, leaving her all alone.

Well! After years of nothing happening, everything was happening at once. She thought about Cook's cozy little cottage full of grandchildren and was rather tempted to go and knock on her door. *You can't, Clara*, she told herself sternly. She could hardly go and foist herself on Cook, not on the very day she'd been sacked.

Clara still had the shiny fifty-pence coin in her pocket that Cook had given her. She would spend it in the café that she'd visited with James! Yes, a cup of tea and a cake while she waited was by far the best idea.

Inside, the café was warm and steamy. The tables were covered in red-and-white checkered cloths, and on each one stood a slim vase holding a frilly pink flower. Clara went to the counter as though she did this sort of thing every day and ordered her tea. She pointed to the largest cake she could see, a Chelsea bun covered in glossy white icing and topped with a cherry so luminous she could imagine it glowing in the dark.

"Is it shoe day already?" asked the lady in a friendly manner. "Where's Mr. James?"

"He's not here," said Clara. "I'm waiting for Uncle. He's gone on some errands, but he'll be back soon." She found a table and surveyed her surroundings. The café really was a very pleasant place: pop music playing on the radio, the hiss and spit of steam rising from the teakettle, colorful cakes piled high on the fancy cake stand, pictures of kittens and puppies decorating the walls.

The hot tea scalded Clara's throat, but it was lovely. The

icing on the bun turned to sweet powder on her tongue. She took her time, savoring every bite and sip while examining the pictures of the puppies and kittens, deciding which one she would have if she were ever allowed a pet. She thought probably the jet-black kitten with the golden eyes. It stared out at her pitifully, as if it were saying "Please take me home."

After Clara had finished her refreshments and sat there for a little while longer, listening to the hum of the customers and the catchy music on the radio, she decided it was probably time to pay and leave. Uncle was taking forever. Maybe she should wait outside. Clara stuck her hand in her pocket to retrieve the fifty-pence coin. But instead of grabbing it, she pulled out a piece of paper folded around a package. Carefully she unfolded it to reveal a thick wad of ten-pound notes. She stared at them in astonishment. Where had they come from? Quickly, she counted them. There were twenty in total, crisp and brown, with a picture of the Queen on one side and a lion on the other. Two hundred pounds!

She was still wondering how they had found their way into her pocket when she noticed the paper they were wrapped in had a note scrawled on the underside. It was written in familiar black spidery handwriting.

Take care. —Uncle

Clara drew in a sharp breath. Had he *abandoned* her? The thought was swift and unexpected, like a cold blade pointing at her throat.

Clara sat at the café table, a maelstrom of thoughts whirling around and around in her head. He must be late because something had happened to him. Maybe he'd had an accident in the car or dropped dead. But the rational part of Clara's brain told her that if that were the case there would have been a commotion, an ambulance—somehow word would have gotten back to the café; she would have known. And if he was coming back, why slip her the money and the note?

Clara gazed at the other people in the café. After they finished here, they had something to do, somewhere else to go. A horrible lump wedged itself into the back of her throat. She tried to swallow it, but it wouldn't budge. Should she tell someone? Maybe the lady behind the counter? She had been friendly. *And* she remembered her from the shoe visits. Or perhaps it was better to choose a parent. A couple was sitting at the next table with a baby in a buggy. But they looked upset, as if they were having an argument, so that wouldn't do.

Anyway, what would she say? "Excuse me, I think my uncle has abandoned me"? Then what would happen? The authorities would take over. She'd be sent to a workhouse or something. Actually, she was pretty sure workhouses didn't exist anymore. But it was bound to be something similar, a terribly cruel orphanage or a harsh boarding school for unwanted children.

Clara stood, the storm of thoughts crowding her head. She felt sick. And a bit dizzy. Walking over to the counter, she paid her bill.

"Where's your uncle, then?" the lady inquired, giving Clara her change.

"I'm meeting him outside," said Clara, surprising herself when the lie just popped out, fully formed.

Outside, it had started to spit with rain. Clara shivered. She didn't have her gloves or a hat. She took the note out of her pocket and read the message again. He really didn't care, not at all. This note was proof of it, right here, in her hands.

Clara stood, gripped by indecision. The rain had started in earnest now, icy needles scratching her skin. *Clara*, she said to herself, *remember what Cook said: "You're a strong 'un. You'll survive."* She would just have to work this out on her own.

And then it came to her, clear as day. No more of the deathly dull routine. No more people telling her what to do. No more being ordered around. Of course she wasn't going to tell anyone! She was going to take charge, go home, and look after herself for a change.

FIVE

FOREVER AND EVER, BRAITHWAITE MANOR HAD just stood there on the moors, dark and inhospitable, as though it were saying "Go away, traveler" rather than "Come in." But it was the only home Clara had ever known, and after the half-hour tramp through whistling wind and lashing rain, when its familiar hulk finally loomed into view, she felt awash with relief. She was soaking wet, her shoes were sodden, and her feet felt like lumps of lead.

It wasn't until she was almost at the door that she noticed the boy. He was trying without much success to shelter under one of the straggly bushes that sprouted from the rock garden, his arms attempting to shield a basket at his feet. "At last!" he cried, leaping up and rushing toward her as she approached. He was small and wiry, with light-colored hair gone muddy brown in the rain. "I've been here forever! Where have you been? And where's Mr. Starling?"

Clara stopped dead in her tracks and stared. Behind the boy was a for-sale sign, its post jammed into the soil at a strange angle as though it were leaning into the wind. This was not part of the plan! She'd come back to live on her own at home. She couldn't do that if the house was to be sold! She looked back at the boy, who was gazing at her with a mixture of impatience and . . . was it hope? She didn't think anyone had looked at her quite like that before.

"Who are you? Did you put this up?" she asked, pointing at the sign. She didn't mean it to sound like an accusation, but that's how it came out.

"Of course I didn't," the boy said indignantly. "I'm Peter Trimble, Apartment 64, North Tower, Kennington, London, SE11. I've been sent here to stay with Mr. Edward Starling while Granny is recuperating. Just for a few weeks until she's better. Didn't you know? It's all been arranged!"

Clara's head spun. Who on earth was Granny and why was he talking about Uncle as if he were a completely normal human being instead of an irresponsible guardian who had abandoned his one and only niece that very afternoon?

She felt angry and confused. She'd been so looking forward to getting home, getting dry, and trying to remember Cook's instructions for boiling eggs and mashing potatoes. Now here was a boy out of nowhere, talking nonsense, and a for-sale sign outside her house. A small part of her wished Peter Trimble would just disappear.

"Uncle didn't say anything," Clara said. "And now he's gone, so we can't ask."

"What do you mean, he's gone? I'm expected! Are you his niece?" The boy was starting to look distraught.

Clara nodded warily.

"Look," he said, "your uncle, Mr. Starling, is our neighbor Stella's old friend. She wrote to him and said I was coming. And now I'm here and he's not! What shall I do?" He looked at the house and then back at Clara as if he didn't quite believe what she was saying. "Aren't there any other grown-ups?"

"No," said Clara.

Peter started gathering his bags.

"What are you doing?" she said.

"Going back to London!" he said. "If your uncle's gone, and the house is for sale, I can't stay, can I? Besides, Granny needs me."

Clara didn't like the sound of that. If he left and went

back to his granny, could she trust him not to go blab-bering to the authorities? All the way home, she had been thinking about everything she was going to do to the house, rearranging the rooms, tackling the repairs. She wouldn't even be able to start if Peter went and told on her.

"But you just said she needs to recuperate!" objected Clara.

Peter flushed scarlet so that the cinnamon-colored freckles sprinkling his nose almost disappeared. "It's what Stella suggested. She's worried social services will think Granny can't look after me properly and split us up. *And* I've gone and made it worse by getting into trouble at school."

"Oh," said Clara. It all sounded very serious. No wonder he seemed upset.

Now Peter Trimble was bending down and muttering to the basket thing at his feet. He looked up at Clara, his features still clouded with worry.

"Can you hurry up and let us in, then?" he said, "Stockwell isn't used to the rain."

"Who?"

"My cat. She's been stuck in this thing all day," the boy was saying. "She's probably starving. I'll come in and feed her, and then I'd better go back."

Clara turned away from the boy so that he couldn't see

her face while she worked out what to do next. She didn't have a key; *that* was the problem. Without a key, and with no one inside to answer the door, how could they get in? She didn't know why, but she felt it was important for him to think that everything was under control.

"Hurry up!" said Peter.

It was pouring rain, and water streamed like a thousand tears down her face, dripping off her nose and trickling down her cheeks to her chin. Clara kicked the rock garden, dislodging a stone, and then without even thinking, picked it up and quickly ran toward the house, hurling it at the pane of glass to the right of the door. The rock smashed through the window like a cannonball, splintering the glass into tiny pieces. Clara's chest swelled.

"What did you do that for?" Peter was on his feet, mouth open. "You can't just go around breaking windows! Hang on, is this *really* your house?"

Clara walked up the steps to examine the jagged hole. She heard him follow her. She tried to imagine what James would do next.

"Can I have your scarf?" she asked Peter. She watched him unfurl it from his neck. It was sopping wet, but it would do the trick. Carefully she wound it like a bandage around and around her hand and up her arm. Then she stuck her scarf-wrapped arm through the hole in the windowpane. The glass crunched under her feet as she shifted position.

"Careful!" said Peter.

She felt around for the lock. Found it. There was a click, and the heavy door swung open.

"We're in!" said Peter. He was impressed, she could tell. Even better, he was grinning, and the grin reached all the way to his eyes.

SIX

AFTER THEY HAD SWEPT UP ALL THE GLASS SO THE cat wouldn't get any in her paws, Clara flew all over the house switching on every single light. Now that the house was hers, she wanted it to glitter like a star on the moor, every window twinkling so it could be seen far and wide.

When she came back down, Peter had let Stockwell out. The cat was jet-black, just like the picture of the kitten in the café. Her soft coat gleamed like licorice, begging to be stroked.

Tentatively, Clara slid her hand over the smooth fur. Uncle had hated pets. Once, one of the governesses had had a pair of pet mice. Their cage had been like a fairground, with wheels and slides and ladders. The mice had been so sweet, tiny and white, and Clara had loved to hold them in her hands and feel their quivering whiskers. But then Uncle had caught her and the governess sharing their supper with them one day, and he'd flown into a rage and ordered them to be destroyed. The governess had shouted, "Over my dead body!" and left with the mice the next day.

"Where *is* your uncle?" asked Peter, showing Clara how to tickle Stockwell under the chin.

"I don't know," answered Clara truthfully. "He dropped me off in the village and never came back. He's been selling all this stuff, and he sacked Cook and our butler, James. I think he might have run away."

"You had a cook *and* a butler?" Peter stared at her in disbelief. He furrowed his brow, which Clara thought made him look like a little pug dog. "Why would he say I could come if he wasn't planning on being here? Where's the phone? I'd better call and tell Stella."

"Please don't!" said Clara, her heart lurching. "I'll be all right on my own!"

"But the house is for sale," said Peter doubtfully. "If your uncle's got money problems, he's going to have to sell it to get himself out of them. Besides, children aren't allowed to live on their own. Adults don't let them."

"Oh, it'll be fine!" said Clara. She wished he wouldn't look so worried. "I've got money to buy supplies. And I just won't answer the door! Honestly, I've had enough of being ordered around and told what to do. I'm going to be in charge for a change." Peter still looked unconvinced. "Has Stockwell been your cat for long?" she asked to change the subject. It sounded like one of the "what to do in polite society" questions a governess had taught her when she was learning etiquette, but it did the trick and Peter brightened.

Stockwell was a rescue cat, he explained, found at the Stockwell subway station in London by someone named Stanley. "I mean," he said, "what sort of owner abandons a tiny helpless kitten in an underground station? Stanley wanted to call the cat-protection people, but I begged him not to." Peter talked and talked. His voice rose and fell, smooth, then staccato, speeding up and slowing down. When he got excited, he talked louder. It was a lovely change from Uncle's dull monotone.

"Stanley sounds nice," said Clara.

"He is. He's the stationmaster," Peter explained, scratching the cat gently between her ears. "He said I could keep her as long as Granny didn't mind. 'Course, Granny *would* have minded if she was well. She always said cats shouldn't live in apartments, especially as our apartment is on the nineteenth floor, but she's sick, so . . . " Peter's voice trailed off, and he turned away from Clara. Then he said fiercely,

"She's been in bed forever. The doctors don't even know what's wrong. They just keep saying she needs rest!"

"So what *did* your granny say?" asked Clara. If she'd brought a cat home out of the blue, Uncle would have hit the roof.

"Nothing, really," said Peter. "She feels guilty 'cause I have to do everything, like make breakfast and supper— and tidy the apartment. Luckily, when I'm at school, Stella comes to make her lunch. Soup, usually."

The cat stretched luxuriously, her paws straight out in front of her and her head down low. It reminded Clara of the yoga one of her governesses had liked to do. When Stockwell had finished stretching, she rolled on her side for Peter to scratch her tummy, then sprang up and trotted after them into the kitchen, brushing against their legs while they searched first for a can opener and then a saucer.

"Why don't you know where anything's kept?" asked Peter. "I thought you lived here."

"Why *should* I know?" retorted Clara, and then before she could help it, she said in an Uncle-ish sort of way, "The kitchen was Cook's domain."

Peter gave her a look, and she didn't blame him; she sounded rude and awful. They both watched Stockwell tuck into her supper. She ate neatly, from the edge of the saucer inward. When everything was gone, she licked the plate until it shone.

After that, Peter wanted to explore. He ran all over the house, along the second floor and the third floor, exclaiming at the vastness of the rooms, poking his head into every corner, opening cupboards and peering out windows, even though it was quite dark. When he discovered the turret, his eyes gleamed. Clara had never been very fond of the winding stairway leading up to the room at the top where there was one narrow window that let in only a sliver of light. Nevertheless, it had occasionally been a place to flee, to get as far away from Uncle as possible, and to quietly fume.

"This is brilliant!" Peter said, shoving his head into the narrow recess of the window and peering out at the inky blackness beyond. "Your house is massive," he said, pulling back into the room, his hair glittering with droplets of rain. "Like something out of a film."

They were both starving now. Back in the kitchen, Clara showed Peter the contents of the pantry.

"I know!" he said, surveying the eggs and the potatoes. "We can play *The Galloping Gourmet.*"

The Galloping Gourmet was a television program that Peter watched with his granny. As you prepared the food, you talked about what you were doing. When the dish was ready, you invited a member of the audience to try it with you and made ecstatic faces when you tasted the first bite. Peter loved cooking programs. "One day I'm going to have a whole cupboard full of herbs and spices, and I'll make things like beef Wellington—"

"And coq au vin," said Clara.

"And shrimp cocktail!" said Peter.

The first part of the game was to run into the kitchen, jump over a chair, and skid to a halt.

"Welcome to *The Galloping Gourmet*!" announced Peter.

Then it was on to the cooking. They filled two pans with water and set them to boil. It took a while to work out how to turn on the electric burners, but eventually they did it *and* managed to keep up a running commentary throughout.

Next, Peter peeled the potatoes, around and around so that the peel dropped to the counter in perfect spirals. *"Poh-TATE-oh, po-TOT-oh,"* he sang. *"Let's call the whole thing off!"* When Clara had picked up the tune and some of the words, she joined in. It was easy to get carried along by Peter's enthusiasm.

While the pans bubbled and spat, and clouds of steam filled the kitchen, Peter and Clara raised imaginary glasses

of wine and shared cooking tips with the "audience." When the potatoes were done, they drained them and mashed them, and then Peter rapped the eggs theatrically on his forehead to crack the shells before peeling them.

"Never tasted anything so delicious in my whole life," exclaimed Clara. And it was true. It was even better than the salt-and-vinegar chip sandwich a governess had once let her try when Uncle was out.

At last, after they had demolished everything and their plates were squeaky clean, Peter leaned back in his chair and propped his feet on the table. "You and Stockwell aren't the only ones to be abandoned," he confided. "I once was, too, and if it weren't for Granny, I don't know what would have happened."

SEVEN

"GRANNY'S NOT MY REAL GRANNY," BEGAN PETER.
"I was left on a train when I was a baby, in a basket on the
12:52 into Charing Cross. The guard took me to lost and
found, and luckily it was Granny's day for cleaning." He
paused dramatically, as if waiting to see what effect his
revelation had on Clara. "She's a cleaner," he continued.
"Thank goodness she knew Mr. Framlingham."

"Who's he?" asked Clara. She could just picture the
squealing baby in the basket, shocked faces peering down
at the poor abandoned little thing.

"Lawyer. Granny cleaned his offices. He arranged it so
she could adopt me. She said it was love at first sight."

Clara sighed. Peter was a real live orphan. It was just like
some of the stories in her favorite books.

"The trouble is," he said, and the little pug frown appeared again, "I meant what I said about social services. That's why Stella thinks it's safer for me to be here. Plus"—the pug frown deepened—"I don't even know if Granny's paying the rent because she hasn't been able to work for a long time. What if they kick us out?"

"Well, you can't go back, then," Clara blurted out. "Not yet anyway. Look . . . " She pushed her chair back and clattered away down the hall, enjoying the sound of her feet on the polished wood floor, imagining Uncle's pained expression at the noise. She delved in her coat pocket for the rolled-up ten-pound notes and then skidded back to Peter. "I told you I've got all this money. We can be orphans together—I think I count as an orphan if my dad doesn't even know I exist—and survive on our own. I'll have to lie low so that the villagers don't know Uncle's gone, but you can go to the shop and get supplies! And when your granny's better, you can go home. And"—a helpful thought struck her—"if you do get kicked out of your apartment, you can come here."

Peter's eyes were like saucers as he looked at the roll of notes in Clara's hand.

"That is a lot of money," he said.

"Two hundred pounds! Uncle gave it to me," said Clara. "It must be guilt money."

There was a little silence while Peter gently stroked the velvety space between Stockwell's ears. "You could buy a cruise with that," he said at last, "or twelve bicycles, or trillions of chocolate bars . . . but what about when the money runs out?"

Clara was about to explain that, if it did, she would start selling some of the house's belongings, just like Uncle had, when a shrill sound made her jump.

"That'll be Stella," said Peter, and Clara realized it was the telephone, which didn't ring very often. "She'll be calling to check if I got here safely."

Quickly, Clara led the way to Uncle's study, standing back to let Peter in. The phone, almost buried under a mountain of papers, continued to ring.

"Well, answer it, then," said Peter.

"No, you answer it," said Clara, who didn't want to admit that she had never answered a phone before.

Peter gave her a look and picked up the receiver, and Clara held her breath, every muscle in her body clenched tight. *"Don't say anything about Uncle,"* she mouthed to Peter. If Peter gave the game away, her plan would be finished.

"Yes, it's me," Peter was saying. "Yes, everything's fine. Is Granny OK? No, no delays . . . Got a taxi straightaway . . .

He can't talk now, he's cooking dinner . . . Yep, bangers and mash . . . but he says to give you his regards and see you soon. OK, bye."

Clara's eyes widened. Bangers and mash! Give you his regards! Maybe having Peter here would be all right, after all.

"I'll stay tonight," Peter said before Clara could get a word in. "And I'll decide tomorrow what to do."

Clara wasn't going to plead. After all, her plan had been to make her own way in the world; she hadn't bargained on Peter being here, and maybe it would be simpler on her own. And yet there was something about Peter that she liked. His chatter for one thing, filling the house like musical notes running up and down a piano; and then the cooking, which wouldn't have been half so fun without his game. And Stockwell.

"Ugh! What's that?" Peter was wiping his head. "Something dripped on me!"

Clara looked up as another drip splashed down, just missing Peter, who had ducked out of the way, and landed instead with a plop by her feet. How could she not have noticed it? A bicycle-wheel-size bulge was sagging from the ceiling, while fat, grayish drips of water fell down to a little puddle on the floor.

"Oh no." Clara breathed out, feeling a stab of panic. "The leak in the governess's bathroom!" She thought of James the butler and the dark circles beneath his eyes; the buckets that he emptied on the hour, every hour. A terrible realization struck her. They hadn't been emptied for two whole days!

Clara tore out of the study, raced up the stairs, thundered down the second-floor corridor, and ran into the governess's bathroom. Sure enough, the steel buckets were full to overflowing, and water sloshed across the floor, lapping at the baseboards.

Visions of water gushing through the house like a tidal wave flashed before Clara's eyes. She couldn't swim. They'd all drown.

"Get another bucket," she shouted at Peter, who had followed her up. "We have to empty them on the hour, every hour." She splashed across the floor and tried to lift one of the buckets, but it was too heavy.

"Where's it coming from?" asked Peter, splashing to meet her and grasping the other side of the bucket so that, together, they were able to heave it up and whoosh the contents into the bathtub.

"From there!" said Clara, pointing at the crack in the pipe.

"Yes," said Peter, "but where is it coming from before it actually appears? The *source* of the leak, I mean."

"I don't know," said Clara. She had asked James that very same question, but he had merely replied that leaks can be mysterious things, which as far as she was concerned meant he didn't know either.

"We need to direct the water into the bath," said Peter. "Where's the hose?"

"I don't know," said Clara again. Was there a hose? The water was dripping at such a rate that the bucket was already a quarter filled.

"We need to stick something over the crack, then," said Peter. "Tape won't work. . . . I know! What about porridge? That dries like glue!"

"No porridge," said Clara. The water was up to her ankles. It was cold.

"It's got to be something that sticks fast." Peter stared worriedly at the bucket. The water had risen to the half-way mark.

Clara thought frantically. There was the plaster, but James had already tried that and it hadn't worked. What else stuck? A vision of the little night table in the governess's room came in a rush. One of the governesses had liked to chew gum before lights out, and underneath the table it was rock hard and bumpy, a legacy of all the gum she'd stuck there because she couldn't be bothered to get out of bed and put it in the trash can.

Clara thrust the bucket at Peter, sloshed out of the bathroom, and ran across the hall. In the governess's bedroom, she yanked open the little drawer under the dressing-table mirror. Lipstick, a single earring, a train ticket, an almost empty tube of hand cream, a bent hair clip, half a packet of mints, and . . . Yes! One, two, three, four, five sticks of gum. Frantically, she tore at the green paper and silver foil wrappers and stuffed three of the sticks into her mouth, chewing and chomping them as fast as she could. Running back to the bathroom, she gave the remaining two to Peter.

"Chew!" she instructed. Once the gum was chewed enough, she spat it into her hands and worked it into the crack on the pipe with her thumbs, pressing and molding it to fill the gaps. When she had finished, Peter did the same. Grabbing her hand, he clamped it over the gum-filled crack. "Hold on," he said, and without another word, he ran from the room. Clara heard him thump down the stairs. She pressed her hand hard against the tacky gum. She could still feel water finding its way through minuscule gaps the gum had not quite managed to cover. Then Peter was back, thrusting more gum at her, this time in yellow wrappers.

"Had it in my bag," he said, shoving five sticks into his mouth at once. Clara's jaws ached, but she chomped as hard and as fast as she could before sticking the gum on the pipe, layering it this time, alternating with gum and the little sheets of silver foil. Then Peter held it with both hands while Clara ran down to James's cupboard in the kitchen hallway.

The shelves were packed neatly with balls of string, dusters, polish, chalk, vinegar, and, right in the back, a large roll of black duct tape. Clara shot back up the stairs and, with Peter's help, wound the tape as tight as she could, around and around the pipe. When she had used up the whole roll, she sat back with a splash on the floor. The water had stopped dripping. Clara exhaled deeply. The house was safe, for now.

∽

They decided to celebrate conquering the flood by building a hideout in the study. Clara had always been envious of Uncle's domain, with its chestnut-brown leather armchairs—all cracked and shiny from years and years of being used—the heavy crimson curtains made from a plush velvet that swished as you drew them close, the crackling fire that cast a warm, flickering glow on everything. Now Clara was determined to rearrange it how she liked.

"Granny would have a fit if she saw this mess!" said Peter,

starting to collect the scattered papers and build them into mountainous piles, which they pushed to the edges of the room.

"Lucky she's not here, then," said Clara, and Peter laughed.

They pushed the four chairs together to make a boatlike bed, fetched the nicest quilts and blankets down from the bedrooms, and made a blazing fire with some of the papers that Clara deemed unimportant. Peter showed Clara how to make a canopy for the bed, positioning two floor lamps and two brooms at the corners of the chairs and then draping an immense dark-blue quilt over the top to make a roof. Climbing into the bed was like entering a blue cave. Through the gaps in the quilt, Clara could see the glow from the firelight. If only they had steaming cups of hot chocolate, it would have been perfect.

Tucked up in the boat-bed, Clara felt like she was queen of the castle. It was all working out. She and Peter had managed to repair the leak on their own. They had cooked their own supper, and it was edible. "I *am* going to stay here," she whispered to Peter as she drifted toward sleep. "It's my home."

EIGHT

THE NEXT MORNING, WITH THE FIRE DEAD IN THE grate, it was freezing cold. Clara hopped out of the boat-bed to turn on the electric heaters, but although they had worked the day before, they wouldn't now. Neither would the lights come on.

"Your uncle hasn't paid the electric," said Peter, and when Clara looked baffled, he explained: "Electricity isn't free. If you don't pay, they cut you off."

"Here, crumple these up, then," Clara said, handing some of Uncle's papers to Peter. They would light another fire. And when it got dark, they would have candles. She had seen boxes of them in James's cupboard.

They set to work twisting and crumpling the paper. When Peter had worked his way through his first pile, he started on the muddle of papers that Uncle seemed to have tossed at random under his desk.

"Look!"

Clara looked. Peter was waggling a postcard at her.

"It's Rome!" he said. "In Italy! I'd love to go there!" The postcard Peter was holding had a picture of the Colosseum on the front. He turned it over and read the message on the back.

"'Dancing Giselle tonight. Wish me luck, x.'"

Peter's eyes shone. "*Giselle!*" And when Clara looked like she didn't have a clue what he was talking about, he added, "It's a ballet about a girl who goes mad with grief and dies of a broken heart."

It turned out Peter knew all about ballet. He was going to be a ballet dancer when he grew up. "Although Trimble hasn't really got a ballet ring to it, does it?" he said. "It'd be much better if it was something like Starling."

Rudolf Nureyev was his hero. Peter told Clara about the "Heroes and Heroines of Our Time" project he'd done at school, and how his teacher had asked the class to stand up one at a time and speak about someone famous they admired. Peter had decided to talk about when Nureyev was in Paris, on tour with the Kirov Ballet, and how the Communists, worried he was mixing with too many French people, tried to trick him into going back to the USSR.

"First the KGB said he had to dance a very, very important performance at the Kremlin, but that didn't fool him, so *then* they told him his mum was at death's door. Luckily Nureyev guessed it was all a pack of lies," Peter explained. "He defected in 1961, and he hasn't been back to the USSR since."

"How do you know all that?" asked Clara, impressed.

"Library," said Peter. "And before she was ill, Granny took me to see him dance Prince Siegfried—that's in *Swan Lake*—on my birthday. We sat high up, right in the back— you need binoculars to see. You should see him jump, Clara. It's magic."

Clara had never set foot inside a school, let alone a classroom full of children. She didn't think she would have the courage to stand up in front of a whole class and speak about anything! But here was Peter, an actual authority on a subject she knew nothing whatsoever about. She was sure the class would have been transfixed as he told them everything he knew about Nureyev.

"I should have kept my mouth shut," said Peter. "Geoffrey Mullings and Steven Pope are always teasing me for being a granny's boy. Now they call me ballet boy. I spat on them in the corridor after, and then we got in a fight."

He clenched his fists angrily as he spoke.

"Oh! Is that why you got in trouble?" asked Clara,

remembering what Peter had said the day before.

But Peter had stopped talking, his face suddenly alert. And then Clara heard something, too. Quickly she dashed to the window and peered out.

A white car had turned into the drive of Braithwaite Manor and, at this very moment, was pulling up in front of the house. A man in a suit hopped out of the driver's seat. He was clutching a clipboard. His jacket flapped in the wind as he moved to open the passenger door.

"I bet that's the real estate agent!" said Peter. "And those people in the back have come to view your house!"

Clara stared at him in disbelief. Already? She'd barely given another thought to the for-sale sign outside the house. But of course Peter was right. The sign was there for a purpose, not for decoration.

For a split second Clara considered marching to the door and telling the unwanted visitors to get in their car and go away. But just as quickly, she realized she couldn't.

She was a child. The questions would start. They would ask what she was doing there and where Uncle was.

A second car door slammed, then another. Peter and Clara backed away from the window. They mustn't be seen.

Clara's mind raced frantically through the house, assessing hiding places. There was the enormous fireplace in the library; the cupboard at the back of the pantry; the room at the top of the turret. No. Too big; too small; too obvious. None of them would do.

Then there was the wardrobe in the spare bedroom on the third floor . . .

With the greatest urgency, she grabbed Peter's arm and pulled him after her, up two flights of stairs, along the corridor, and into the room at the end.

"In there!" she instructed, gesturing toward a wardrobe so large it towered over the whole room. They had barely crushed themselves inside when they heard the front door open and, moments later, the distant sound of voices float up the stairs.

It was a brilliant hiding place. They would never be found. And yet Clara sensed Peter's whole body go rigid beside her.

"What's wrong?" she hissed. She couldn't hear anything now except for her own heart pounding. The visitors must be at the back of the house.

"We forgot Stockwell!"

"You can't get her now."

"Clara! I must! There, listen!"

Very faintly she heard a mew. Peter pushed open the door of the wardrobe and started to climb out.

Now she could hear the intruders again. Moving from one room to another. The dining room, the study, back into the hall.

Clara tried to grab Peter's leg and yank him back. "Stay here! They're coming!"

But Peter jerked his leg out of Clara's grasp and disappeared into the room. Clara could hear the steady drone of voices now. The creak of feet on the stairs. A door opening somewhere below, then shutting again. Her bedroom? Or Uncle's? Peter was still scurrying around.

"Peter," she whispered. Did he want to get caught? At last the wardrobe door wrenched open and Peter squashed back in, Stockwell in his arms. Clara breathed out. Just in time.

More creaks, even louder now. Footsteps moving along the third-floor corridor. Voices audible outside the spare bedroom door.

". . . Vandalism. Quite unheard of in these parts. Although there are a few undesirables in the next village, children with nothing better to do, you know. Anyway, not to worry, we'll get the door fixed pronto."

"So it's only been on the market for a couple of days then, Gilmore?" A voice with a harsh rasp, metal on metal, like a knife perhaps, scraping against a cheese grater. It made the hairs on the back of Clara's neck stand on end.

"Yes, Mr. Morden. But you'll need to act fast. We've already had several inquiries. It's a prime piece of property. Crying out to be developed."

Gently, Clara shifted her position so that Peter's elbow didn't stick in her ribs quite so much. Stockwell, angry at being in such a confined space when there was a whole house to explore, struggled to escape Peter's grasp.

"Entrez." The sound of several people tramping in. "This is one of the smaller rooms. Fine views across the moors, windows a bit on the petite side, but—I'm sure you'll agree—that's easily fixed."

"Small windows are good." A female voice, stony, cold.

"Suitable for our purposes, eh?" said the cheese-grater voice. "No distractions, no peering eyes."

"Indeed, Morden," said the female voice. "Considering the property comes with . . . *special inclusions*, shall we say . . ."

It was then, as if she wanted to be part of the conversation, that Stockwell meowed.

Clara froze. Had they heard? On the other side of the wardrobe, there was silence.

"Morden!" It was the stone-cold female voice again. Clara's skin prickled. The person sounded very near. "What in hellfire was that?"

NINE

STOCKWELL MEWED AGAIN SOFTLY.

"Is that a cat? We need to go. Mrs. Morden is highly allergic. You'll need to fumigate this place if you want to make a sale . . ."

There was the sound of hurried shuffling, and then the voices became fainter and fainter until they faded away.

For a minute, Clara and Peter remained hunched in the wardrobe listening to the footsteps receding down the stairs, the front door slamming shut, the gravel crunching outside. It was a relief when an engine revved and a screech of tires indicated the car and its passengers had sped away.

"He can't sell this house!" yelled Clara, bursting out of the wardrobe. "I won't let him." She felt outraged, but she was scared, too. What would she do if the house was sold?

Where would she go? She pictured herself, a huddled figure, homeless, dressed in rags and wandering the wild and windy moors for all eternity.

Clara ran to the window, her eyes following the car as it grew smaller and smaller until it was just a speck on the moor. There by the gate was the for-sale sign, announcing that her home was up for grabs. When she'd seen it yesterday, she hadn't quite believed what that meant. Now she knew.

"I'll buy it!" she said, turning to Peter.

"What, with two hundred pounds?" Peter laughed.

"It's my house, too, not just Uncle's. I can sell some of the furniture. And there're still some paintings left!"

She hoped she would never meet the cheese-grater man and the stone-cold woman again. They gave her the shivers. "Well done, Stockwell!" she shouted as the cat streaked out of the room. "I'll get a whole army of cats to keep that lady and her stupid allergy away if I have to."

Clara stomped downstairs, followed by Peter, who slid down the banister.

"Come on," she said. "We've got a job to do."

For the second time that day, she opened James's cupboard. She took out a saw, a jam jar full of nails, and a short plank of wood left over from when James had replaced some rotten floorboards. To Peter, she gave a tin of white paint and a paintbrush.

Outside, Clara blew on her hands to warm them up, then, grasping the wooden handle of the saw in both hands, started to rhythmically saw at the base of the for-sale sign. Back and forth she went, not hacking, but patiently, until the teeth of the saw sliced a groove, going deeper and deeper until—*crack*—there was a splintering sound, and the post keeled over onto the ground.

"Voilà!" she said.

"How d'you know how to do that?" asked Peter admiringly. "In woodwork at school, they won't let us use the saws 'cause of health and safety. Teacher has to do it."

"James taught me," said Clara, kicking the felled post triumphantly. She had the same feeling she'd had when she'd thrown the stone at the window. Proud and brave and strong.

"You any good at painting letters?" she asked Peter.

He was. Clara watched while he painted NOT FOR SALE in neat white script on the short plank of wood. Then she showed him how to bang nails in, and they nailed the sign to the front door.

They were admiring their handiwork when, from inside the house, they heard the phone ringing.

"Stella again?" asked Clara.

She remembered that yesterday Peter had said he would decide today whether he was going home or not. He was proving to be quite useful. She would miss him if he went.

"You answer it," said Peter. "If it is, say I'm helping your uncle in the garden and I can't come to the phone."

"But Uncle never goes in the garden," said Clara.

"Well, say I'm helping him do the vacuuming."

Clara burst out laughing. "But Uncle doesn't do—"

"Oh, Clara, it doesn't matter!" interrupted Peter. "Just say your uncle and I are busy. If Stella knows we're on our own, she'll worry, and I bet you anything she'd be on the next train here."

Amazingly, the phone was still ringing when they reached it. *Stella must be very keen*, Clara thought as she picked up the receiver and pressed it to her ear. The plastic was cold against her skin.

"Hello?"

"Can I speak to Mr. Starling, please?" The voice on the other end of the line was male.

"He's not here," said Clara. She didn't know what else to say. Peter was frantically mouthing something at her, but she couldn't tell what.

"Do you know when he'll be back?"

"Soon, I should think," she said.

"Ask, 'Who's calling please?'" whispered Peter.

"Who's calling, please?" she repeated into the receiver.

"Jackson Smith," the voice said. "Tell him I'll call back this afternoon."

There was a click and then a buzzing noise. Clara put the receiver back on its cradle.

"Someone named Jackson Smith," she told Peter. "Whoever that is."

"Might be a debt collector," said Peter.

"Or another house buyer."

"Or someone from the authorities who's been tipped off that you might be on your own."

Very deliberately, Clara unplugged the phone and wound the spiraling cord into a neat loop. "There. Now we won't have to answer it anymore," she said.

"I'm starving," said Peter, "but not for more eggs and potatoes. Can I have some of that money, and I'll go into the village for supplies?"

Clara felt a rush of relief at his words. All of a sudden, she knew without a shadow of doubt that she wanted him to stay. She thought they might become friends—he'd be the first real friend she'd ever had.

So Clara unrolled her stash of notes and gave Peter

several. She drew a map showing him how to walk across the moor to the village. They agreed he wouldn't speak to anyone apart from polite conversation in the shop. Stockwell would stay with Clara.

After Peter had gone, the house seemed very quiet, and Clara appreciated the cat's company. It was the first time she had ever been truly alone in the house. Of course she'd *felt* alone before, but it wasn't quite the same. She stroked the cat's inky-black fur thoughtfully, feeling excited and happy. She had made it clear that the house was not for sale. No one could phone them. For now, they were safe.

She started thinking about what she could do for Peter that was nice, something to show that she wanted to be his friend. She wanted to show that she understood his worries, about his granny being ill and the rent and the electric and stuff like that. She decided she would do something to make him smile.

In Cook's odds-and-ends drawer, she found scissors, a needle, and thread. In her bedroom, she rummaged in her wardrobe and drew out an old dress that had fit perfectly last summer but was now too small.

Clara pulled the old dress apart at the seams and then sewed it back together much smaller. She wasn't very good with the needle and bloodied her fingers and the fabric quite a bit, but the red specks blended quite nicely with the rose print of the fabric, so it didn't matter. A cat dress! With the leftover material, she made a sort of mobcap. Then she picked Stockwell up and dressed her. The cat didn't struggle one bit and looked darling.

Clara had been so involved with her sewing that she hadn't noticed the time. Now she saw it was past two in the afternoon. Peter had been gone for hours! Her mind raced ahead, assessing several nightmare scenarios. Perhaps he had been killed on the moors by a mad ax murderer, or worse, he had gone back to London without telling her.

But just as she was trying to work out what course of action she should take, the door slammed downstairs.

"I'm home!" shouted Peter. "And I've got loads of food!" He had gotten lost on the moors, he complained, because the map had been useless. But when Stockwell scampered down the stairs in her new dress and cap, he burst out laughing, and Clara felt a small surge of pride.

Much later, after they had gorged on a feast of new potatoes and fish in tomato sauce eaten straight from their tins, followed by gallons of something utterly delicious called butterscotch instant whip, Clara made a fire in the study with a whole *Roget's Thesaurus* and half a Russian dictionary. With no electricity, they lit scores of candles.

The flickering fire cast a warm glow on everything, and snuggling down in her boat-bed, with Stockwell tucked in beside her, Clara felt infused with happiness.

But Peter let out a long, shuddery sigh.

"What's the matter?" Clara asked.

"Nothing," said Peter. And then, "Well, if you must know, I'm a bit homesick. Don't laugh."

"I'm not!" said Clara. They were top to tail, and her eyes were level with Peter's feet, which looked small and sort of helpless in his stripy socks. There was a hole in the left one, and his big toe was sticking out.

"I've never been away from Granny before," said Peter. "Maybe I *should* go back tomorrow."

Please don't, Clara thought.

"What does homesick feel like?" she asked.

"Like a sort of hollow in your heart." Peter sniffed.

Clara was quiet for a moment. *A hollow in your heart.* The words described perfectly a feeling she'd had for so long it felt normal.

"Peter, I've been thinking," she whispered. "We're both the same, aren't we? Our pasts are sort of a dead end. Wouldn't you like to know about your real mum and dad?"

"No, I would not!" The words came out fierce and fast. "Why would I want to find out anything about the people who dumped me? They didn't want me, so I don't want them!"

Clara supposed that made sense. She lay there for a while, snuggled in her quilt, cozy and quiet.

"It's just," she said, "if my father doesn't know I exist, he can't know if he wants me or not, can he?"

But all she got in reply was a gentle snore.

TEN

THEY WERE EATING GIGANTIC BOWLS OF SUGAR puffs for breakfast when there was a knock at the door. Clara froze. "We can't answer it," she said. "What if it's Mr. and Mrs. Morden again?"

There was another knock. Then the sound of the letter-box flapping and a voice calling "*Coo-eeee!*" floating down the hallway and into the kitchen where they sat. It was a high, clear voice. It didn't *sound* sinister, thought Clara.

"*Coo-eeee!*" There it was again.

"What if it's a trick?" said Peter.

"Let's go and see," said Clara. "We don't have to open the door if we don't want to."

They edged out of the kitchen and along the hall, keeping close to the walls. When they got to the front door,

Clara peered through a gap in the cardboard that they had used to cover the broken window. It was hard to see properly, but she could just about make out a girl with wild red hair and, behind her, a boy who was walking on his hands, around and around in circles. Beyond him was a small girl clinging to the front leg of a muscular-looking horse. A horse?!

"Who are you?" Clara shouted through the letterbox. "What do you want?"

"Amelia-Ann," shouted the girl with red hair, coming closer to the door. "And these are my cousins, Lucille and Curtis. And that's Dapple." The horse whinnied. "We've come to ask if you want to play."

This was unexpected. "How do I know you're not from the authorities?" yelled Clara. "Or the real estate agents?"

The girl came right up to the letterbox so her eyes were level with Clara's, merely inches away. They were startling eyes, like bright-blue buttons. Clara was pretty sure they were twinkling, if that were possible.

"We're children, not authorities or real-estate-agent thingies!" The girl laughed. "Your cook is our Nanny Poll. We've wanted to play here forever, but Nan always said your uncle wouldn't like it. But yesterday we followed your friend back, and we guessed you were all alone."

Cook's grandchildren! And the girl had described Peter as her friend! "They followed you!" she said to Peter.

Now Peter shouted through the letterbox, "You were spying on me!"

Clara noticed his fists were clenched. Gently, she nudged him.

"Peter, I think it's OK."

She opened the door, and the girl called Amelia-Ann bounded in.

"Look at all this!" she shrieked. "I always knew it would be like a palace in here!"

She was dressed in a yellow mackintosh, thick black tights, and white high-heeled shoes that were several sizes too big. She was gazing around in wonderment, as though she had never seen anything like it before.

"D'you like them?" she asked, noticing Clara's eyes on her shoes. She stuck out her ankle rather elegantly for Clara to admire. "They're Tom's girlfriend's. She works at Lewis's in Leeds."

Clara had no idea who Tom was, or what Lewis's was, but she knew it must have been good because the girl was looking at her as though she expected her to be impressed.

Amelia-Ann shrugged off her coat to reveal a ribbed turtleneck and a pleated skirt, both black. "Pleased to meet you both," she said, twirling around in a circle and then sticking out her hand first to Clara and then to Peter. "Mam says if redheads haven't got anything in green, they should wear black. Come on, Dapple, come on, Luci and Curtis."

The horse ducked its head neatly, politely minding the door frame, as though it visited strange houses every day. It clip-clopped into the hall and stood there expectantly, shuffling its feet and looking at Clara as if waiting for her to say "How do you do?"

"We're staying with Nan 'cause our mum's gone to Trinidad to see her sister," said Curtis. He, too, held his hand out for Clara and Peter to shake. Clara stared at his hair. It was the best hair she had ever seen, like a black halo.

"Dad works nights," added Lucille helpfully. She had a very deep voice for someone so small, thought Clara. She was dressed in a grubby princess costume, pink and gauzy, that sparkled in places and was so long it puddled on the floor. Her hair hung down her back in thousands of fine braids. "D'you *both* live here, then?" She looked from Clara to Peter. "We've come to play sardines."

"Manners, Luci!" admonished Amelia-Ann.

Lucille stuck out her hand. "How d'you do, nice to meet you, thanks for having us," she said in a rush. "NOW can we play sardines?"

Clara felt almost giddy with excitement. She was actually face-to-face with the children she had heard so much about! She was about to say yes, even though she had no idea what sardines was, when she felt Peter tugging at her arm and saw that the pug frown was back on his face.

"Clara, can I talk to you in private?"

"What's the matter?" Clara asked when they were in the other room, out of earshot.

"How do we know they're telling the truth?" asked Peter. "What if they go back and tell someone you're here on your own?"

"But they are telling the truth! Cook's name *is* Polly. I know Luci and Curtis live in Leeds. Their mum's a nurse, and their dad—"

"Test them," said Peter, "just to be sure."

"Amelia-Ann," Clara yelled through the door, "where does your mum work and what's her name?"

"Cruise ship," came the answer. "Babs."

"See!" she said.

"Get a move on," Amelia-Ann shouted. "We want to start the game!"

"OK?" Clara looked at Peter. She needed him to want this, too.

He nodded, and she breathed an inner sigh of relief.

"Only because I've never played it in a house this size before," he said.

Clara opened the door, and they went back out into the hall where the three visitors and the horse were waiting.

"You can stay," she said, "but you have to promise—"

"Swear on your life—" added Peter.

"That you won't tell. Not Cook—I mean Nanny Poll—Polly—or anybody."

"Cross our hearts and hope to die," said Amelia-Ann, putting her hand to her heart and gazing at them both with appropriate solemnity. She clapped her hands imperiously. "Now, Curtis, show Peter your gymnastics!"

Curtis jumped three times on the balls of his feet, flipped backward onto his hands, and then leaped up into a standing position, his chest thrust out and his arms aloft. Amelia-Ann and Lucille cheered. He did a double somersault in the air, and they all cheered again, even Peter.

And then the horse, as though he were feeling left out, did his own showpiece, very deliberately, depositing three enormous portions of horse dung on the polished floor.

"Dapple!" shrieked Amelia-Ann. "It's OK to do that at home, but not here! We're visitors!"

For a minute there was a stunned silence, and then Clara was looking at Amelia-Ann, who was looking at her, and it was something about the girl's button eyes looking so shocked, almost as shocked as her crazy red hair, that struck a chord inside Clara. Then she was snorting and laughing as though a tap had been turned on, and her laughter was gushing out in one unstoppable torrent, and Amelia-Ann was laughing, and so were Peter and Curtis and Lucille.

Clara had never laughed like this in her life before, and now she couldn't stop. She laughed so much her sides ached, and then her tummy hurt and she had to lie on the floor, and that made everyone laugh even more.

At last, when the laughter had turned to hiccups, and Clara's body had gone all weak, as though she'd just completed a marathon, they started to play.

"Fists out," said Peter. Clara stood in a circle with the rest of them, both fists stuck out as Peter tapped each with his own, reciting: "One potato, two potato, three potato, four, five potato, six potato, seven potato, more." On the "more," Peter's fist landed on Curtis's, who responded by putting one of his fists behind his back. Peter carried on counting, knocking his own fist on his chin when it was his turn. Around and around he went, and each time he landed on "more" another fist disappeared behind a back. Finally, only one person—Lucille—was left with a fist sticking out. It meant she was the first to hide.

"Scat!" shouted Amelia-Ann, and Lucille shot off, while the others all shut their eyes and counted to twenty. Then, "Coming, ready or not!" yelled Curtis, and they raced from room to room, hunting their prey.

It took a long time to find Lucille, even though all she had done was creep between the sheets in Uncle's room and lie there still as a statue, flat as a pancake. There were so many covers and comforters on the bed that Clara had barely noticed a gentle quivering. But when she finally pulled back the covers, there were Lucille and Curtis and Amelia-Ann, stifling giggles, silently gesturing at Clara to be quiet so Peter wouldn't hear, and Clara had climbed in, too, and held her breath until Peter finally found them.

They played all afternoon, and Clara felt alive, like a kind of fire was surging through her and she was seeing the house for the first time. There were cupboards every-where—no longer just boring spaces to store stuff, but dark, secret places, promising concealment. Under the stairs, in the pantry, below the bookshelves on the second- and third-floor hallways. There were so many hiding places: vast wardrobes, deep chests, voluminous curtains, nooks and crannies revealing themselves at every turn, perfect for squeezing into and huddling quiet as mice.

The children, like Peter, were mad for the turret.

Amelia-Ann wanted to play Rapunzel, but her hair wasn't long enough. Lucille wanted a flashlight so she could switch it on and off and play lighthouses. "Let's pretend the moor is the sea," she said in her husky voice. "I'm the lighthouse keeper, and I've got to stop the ships crashing on the rocks!"

Later, after Peter had shown them how he could wiggle his ears—and the only other one who could do it was Clara—Amelia-Ann wanted to redecorate, so they fetched Clara's felt pens and colored in the pale squares where the paintings had once hung at intervals up the stairs.

After that, they took turns riding Dapple on a circuit through the library, hall, and dining room. When it was Curtis's turn, he stood on the horse's back like a circus performer. They pushed the furniture in the dining room right up against the walls, and Curtis taught Peter how to do a cartwheel, then a headstand, and then a handstand with both him and Amelia-Ann holding his ankles. After that, they all practiced backbends, and Curtis showed Peter how to flip down from a handstand to a backbend and then spring up again.

It was while they were sliding down the banisters, and Peter had disappeared with Curtis into the kitchen to mix up a giant bowl of butterscotch instant whip, that there came a sharp knock at the door.

Amelia-Ann's eyes widened. "Don't answer it," she hissed. While they'd been decorating the stairs, Clara had told her all about the real estate agent and the sinister-sounding couple. "Just ignore it, and they'll go away." There was another loud rap. Shuffles and mutterings. The blurry outline of someone tall and thin.

"Anyone home?" the blurry outline called. It was a man. More mutterings. More shuffling. Then the letterbox flapped, and a card fluttered through and wafted down onto the floor.

As soon as they were certain the visitor had left, Clara scuttled forward and picked the card up. "'Jackson Smith Esq.,'" she read. "'Private Investigator.'"

Jackson Smith! It was the very same man who had telephoned yesterday to speak to Uncle.

Amelia-Ann's eyes looked as though they were about to pop. "What's he investigating?"

"I don't know," said Clara. "But if he wants to take the house away from me, I won't let him."

"*We* won't let him," said Amelia-Ann as she grasped Clara's hand.

They ate the instant whip in the kitchen and traded ideas about how to keep the house safe. Curtis wanted to make a barricade. Amelia-Ann wanted to go to the newspapers and get someone to write a story about it with photos, but Peter pointed out that that would have the opposite effect. They mustn't draw attention to Clara's newfound independence. She had to lie low.

"Sawing down the for-sale sign wasn't enough," Peter said. "We need to take the house off the market." He screwed up his forehead in what Clara now recognized as his thinking face. "I know! Plug the phone back in, Clara."

Peter's idea was brilliant. Within minutes, they had found a telephone directory in Uncle's study and located the number of the real estate agent. Then Lucille had put on her deepest voice and announced herself as Edward Starling. "I've changed my mind," she boomed in an impressive baritone. "I no longer want to sell the house."

Looking around at her friends, Clara had a renewed sense of hope. Her plan was going to work. With everyone's help, she really would be able to fend for herself.

ELEVEN

*E*VEN THOUGH PETER SAID IT WAS BOUND TO BE
only until the grown-ups found out, Clara was over-
joyed that the imminent danger of the house being sold
had passed.

When Uncle had been in charge, Braithwaite Manor
had just been the bare bones of a house, a skeleton without
feeling or warmth. Now with Peter in it, and with Cook's
grandchildren coming to play, it felt like a living, breathing
thing, a place with hope and heart. *What a proper family
home must feel like,* thought Clara.

And Peter seemed happier, too.

The garden and the moors beyond, which had seemed so
desolate before, were now alive with possibility. Peter and
Clara spent hours chalking hopscotch on the paving stones

near the straggly rose beds; whacking tennis balls they'd found in James's cupboard against the walls; making their own miniature gardens with moss and broken tiles.

When Cook's grandchildren came around, they'd race out onto the moor and play kick-the-can, or make pies out of mushed-up mud and heather. If it was too cold, or if it rained, they'd rush back into the house and thunder up the winding stairs to the turret. Here they'd sit in a circle, with Stockwell at their center, and Peter would boast about the games he played in London, mucking about in dumps and lighting firecrackers in alleys—and knockdown ginger, which meant knocking on people's front doors and running away before they'd opened them. It sounded exciting, Clara thought. But she was also starting to understand why Peter was always getting into trouble at school.

One of Amelia-Ann's favorite things to do was talk. She liked to lounge on Clara's bed and ask endless questions. One day, while the others practiced gymnastics downstairs, they had just moved on from their favorite names ("Elisabeth with an S" for Amelia-Ann; Adelaide for Clara) to the Rapunzel braid that Amelia-Ann had begged Cook to knit out of old fishing nets, when they heard a plaintive meow.

"Stockwell?" called Clara. "Is that you?" The meow came again. It wasn't an "I want feeding" meow or even an "I want to be stroked" meow. It was a "worried, maybe even a little scared" meow.

"Stockwell?" Clara tried again. Where was she? Something scratched by her feet. But there was nothing there. A scrabble. A whimper. Clara bent down and put her ear to the ground. She heard a little meow again. Somehow, the cat had gotten herself stuck under the floorboards.

"Peter!" Clara yelled, "Stockwell's trapped!"

Peter cantered up the stairs. "How did she get down there?" he cried. "There must be a hole somewhere." So they ran up and down the second-floor corridor and in and out of every room, looking and looking, calling and calling, first loud, then soft and coaxing. If they could only find the hole, they could persuade Stockwell to climb back out.

"If she got down there, she'll be able to get back up," Clara tried to reassure Peter. But Peter looked stricken, his face pale, his freckles standing out in tiny specks of shock.

"You don't understand!" he said, his voice wavering. "She's a rescue cat. Being down there in the dark will remind her of being lost in the London Underground. She'll think she's been abandoned all over again!"

"Stockwell, Stockwell!" They heard another meow. It *was* coming from Clara's bedroom. They rushed back in, and there by the radiator pipe was a tiny hole, about the size of an eggcup, and a little velvet nose pressed pitifully up toward the gap.

Peter got down on the floor so his face loomed over the hole. The cat meowed sadly. She was small, but not small enough to fit through a hole that size.

"Oh, Stockwell," said Peter. "It's all right, we'll get you out of there."

"I could take the floorboard up," said Clara. She couldn't bear seeing Peter looking so wretched. So she fetched a chisel and a hammer and, after a lot of huffing and puffing and getting it wrong, eventually managed to prize the board open and carefully pull out the nails from the joists. Then she and Curtis lifted the board up, and there was Stockwell, covered in a fine layer of dust and looking like she'd had a fright and gone gray overnight.

"What on earth have you got there?" Peter crooned as he gently lifted her out and cradled her in his arms. Clamped between her teeth was a bedraggled length of ribbon attached to a crumpled piece of dirty pink satin.

Gently, Peter extricated the fabric and smoothed it out.

"A ballet shoe," he said, his eyes alight. "You never told me you did ballet, Clara!"

"I don't," said Clara.

Peter had taken off his sneaker and was trying to stuff

his foot into the shoe. It had definitely seen better days. It was more gray than pink, slippery and soft.

The shoe didn't fit, but Peter pointed his foot in a ballet-type way anyway. He did look quite graceful, Clara thought. "This person had very small feet," he said, tugging it off and turning it over in his hands. "Look, there's something on the sole."

It was gloomy in the house with no electricity and no sun shining in, so Peter carried the shoe over to the window where it was a tiny bit brighter. Clara leaned in. Just about legible was a number and a name: 028658, PETRUSCHKA.

"We know that place, don't we, Luci?" said Curtis. "It's a shop in Leeds! On the street where the Brass Kettle is."

Clara felt a kind of electric thrill course up and down her body. A mystery in her very own house! "We've got to go there!" she said. "Peter, d'you remember the postcard you found in the study? The one from the person dancing Giselle in Rome? Maybe *that* was who wore this shoe! Now we can find out!"

"It's your lucky day," said Amelia-Ann with an extremely satisfied smile. "Tom's driving Luci and Curtis into Leeds this afternoon."

"We're going home for a few days 'cause our dad isn't working nights," her cousin Luci explained.

"We'll ask Tom to drop us off on the way," said Amelia-Ann, "and then we can go to the ballet shop."

∽

Tom was Amelia-Ann's big brother, and he drove a red Ford Cortina. Peter sat in the front with Stockwell, holding the ballet shoe so the cat could bat at the ribbons with her paws. Clara squished in the back with the others. Amelia-Ann wore a furry jacket that looked like it might once have been a rabbit, and her hair protruded in a sort of palm tree on top of her head.

Tom, all arms and legs in faded denim, folded himself into the driver's seat. A single gold earring glinted in his ear. He looked questioningly at the cat.

"I told you . . ." said Amelia-Ann. "This is Stockwell."

"Named after the subway station," confirmed Peter.

"Cool," said Tom, revving the engine loud.

Tom drove fast, the music turned up so high that Stockwell leaped into the back. Luci shared coconut drops, dark syrupy jewels that tasted like coconut and ginger. Peter rolled the window down even though it was freezing and sat with his elbow out, moving his head to the music and clicking his fingers. Amelia-Ann wound her scarf around both herself and Clara, so they were tied together "like two peas in a pod!" and asked Clara a stream of questions like she usually did.

As the car sped along and the wind rushed in from the open window, Clara sucked her candy and brushed her hair out of her eyes. The rock music was pounding so hard she could almost feel it in her chest. She had never heard anything like it before. A voice soared high above the guitars and drums, lonely and desolate, just like the moor. Amelia-Ann locked little fingers with her. "Friends forever," she whispered. And then the wide expanse of purple moor shrank back and gave way to the houses and streets of outer Leeds; the sounds of the city filled the air, and the car slowed to join the snaking lines of traffic along the busy thoroughfares.

"Where d'you want to be dropped off?" bellowed Tom.

"Main drag," yelled Amelia-Ann from the back. "We can cut through one of the department stores," she said to Clara. "Wander around a little before the ballet shop."

Tom swerved sharply right, ignoring the indignant toots from the oncoming cars, and pulled to a stop with a screech.

"Be here at five or make your own way back," he said to Amelia-Ann as Curtis and Luci shrieked goodbyes to Clara and Peter.

"See you next week," they cried.

"And don't get up to any of your tricks," added Tom, "or I'll tell Nan."

"Blah blah blah, and anyway, how will you know if I do?" said Amelia-Ann.

Clara imagined what would have happened if she had spoken to Uncle like that. But Tom didn't explode or even say one mean thing. Instead he laughed, tweaked Amelia-Ann's palm-tree hair, and gave her some coins. "Scram! And don't forget to get everyone cream buns."

When Clara and James had come on their expeditions to Leeds, they'd always gone straight to the shoe shop and, once that mission was accomplished, headed back home. Window-shopping was the opposite. It was all about lingering. So while Peter took Stockwell off to look at the pet department, Amelia-Ann and Clara swanned about, spraying each other with perfume, wrapping themselves in feather boas, and pulling on plum-colored suede boots.

Later, they all met in the café on the fifth floor where they tucked into ginormous round buns, light as air and oozing with cream and jam. Stockwell sat on Peter's lap, her little black head peering just above the table.

"I'm SO glad we're friends now," Amelia-Ann declared. "Tom's going back to college next week, and Luci and Curtis won't be around so much when Auntie Celeste comes back. It's boring as anything with just Nan."

"What about your mum?" Clara pictured Amelia-Ann's

mum, Babs, dancing her way around the world on a cruise ship. She must be impossibly glamorous. Amelia-Ann would be glamorous, too, when she grew up.

"She's hardly ever here," said Amelia-Ann. She jabbed her cream bun with her finger and watched the jam ooze out. "She prefers being at sea—says she hasn't got land legs."

They were all mum-less, thought Clara. Peter's mum had left him on a train. Clara's mum had died. Amelia-Ann's mum preferred being on a ship to being at home.

"What tricks was Tom talking about?" asked Peter.

Amelia-Ann smiled, and her eyes brightened.

"Promise you won't tell?" she whispered.

"Promise," they both said together.

"Look."

Clara and Peter craned their necks to see what Amelia-Ann had taken out of her pocket and was now holding under the table. Two shiny bottles of nail polish—one turquoise, one canary yellow—glittering like jewels in her hand.

"Did you take it?" exclaimed Clara.

"*Shh*, keep your voice down," said Amelia-Ann. But it was too late. An official-looking man was bearing down on them. He had a scowl on his face and was dressed in a uniform.

TWELVE

"QUICK!" SHOUTED AMELIA-ANN, THROWING HER bun down so it landed with a splat, the cream and jam sticking it to the table. "Scat!"

For a split second, Clara's eyes met Peter's, and then she was hurling her bun down, scraping back her chair, and running, streaking after Amelia-Ann out of the café, through the soft furnishings department, past kitchenware and down the staircase, down, down, out onto the ground floor, past the cosmetics stands and onto the street.

"Keep going!" yelled Amelia-Ann over her shoulder.

Clara's heart felt like it was in her throat, her ears pounding. She ran behind Peter and Stockwell and Amelia-Ann, down a side street, into an alley, up a flight of stairs leading to another alley, and onto another narrow street. At last

Amelia-Ann stopped, heaving great gulping breaths. The three of them collapsed in a huddle on the pavement, shaking with a combination of relief and laughter.

"You shouldn't . . ." started Clara. But Peter was turning out his pockets now. "This was all I could get," he said, holding out a small red net bag full of glassy-eyed marbles and a tiny pen light. He flashed the light on and off. "You should see what I *usually* get. You wouldn't believe how easy it is to shove a model plane into your schoolbag in Woolworth's," he added. And then, with a spurt of laughter, he said, "Although they did catch me the time before last. I was in my school uniform, and they told the headmaster. He went mad."

Clara didn't know whether to be shocked or impressed. Stockwell peeped out at her from the inside of Peter's jacket. She was looking at Clara as if to say *What are you waiting for? You've got important business to attend to.* "Let's go and find Petruschka," Clara said.

The street Amelia-Ann led them to was crowded with a jumble of small shops: a tobacconist with an array of pipes in the window; a stick maker full of walking sticks and umbrellas; a tiny, rickety shop selling small silver things—pill cases and thimbles and teaspoons and charms. Petruschka was toward the end of the street, squashed between The Button Box and Books for Keeps.

Clara's skin tingled.

The shop was lit by hundreds of twinkling lights, and dozens of ballet shoes danced across the window display. There were scarlet ones with little bows, plain black-leather ones with elastic straps, and satin ones in the palest pink and ivory, slippery ribbons pinned to look like they were fluttering. BALLET SHOES, EVERY STYLE, MADE TO MEASURE, read a small card at the front of the display. BY APPOINTMENT ONLY. PLEASE RING THE BELL.

"If I can't be a ballet dancer when I grow up, I'm going to have a shop like this!" said Peter, passing the ballet shoe over to Clara and jabbing at the bell.

The satin slipper felt light and insubstantial. Unlike the shoes in the window, each one with a partner, this one was on its own. It was a forlorn little scrap, but there was something precious about it all the same.

"What's this, then, what's this? Can't you read? Card says by appointment only." The door opened, and an elderly man peered out. He had a brush of snowy-white hair held back by gold-rimmed glasses perched high on his head. At his neck was a neat bow tie printed with tiny bluebirds.

"We're sorry—" started Clara. But in spite of what he said, the man was already ushering them in and retreating behind a glass-topped counter under which were displayed dozens of ribbons of various shades and widths. Shoe-size drawers lined the walls of the shop, each one labeled in minuscule writing. Music was playing, filling the room, dipping and soaring. Behind the counter were photographs of dancers—some in full costume, others in practice clothes—many of them scrawled with signatures and kisses. There was a stool in the corner that Amelia-Ann perched on, her hands underneath her bottom as though she didn't trust them to not swipe something. Peter stood alert, almost quivering. Clara could see that he was entranced.

"You want shoes for your ballet lessons, eh, children?" said the man. "Let's measure you up, then. Who's first?"

"No, no," said Clara quickly, "that's not what we are here for." Carefully she placed the lonely ballet slipper on the counter. All five of them regarded it, Stockwell rather disdainfully, as though she'd had absolutely nothing to do with it over the last few hours.

"I'm afraid we don't do repairs," said the man, a look of concern passing over his features. "We used to, but now it's just me . . ."

"It's not that," said Clara. "We found this shoe, and we wondered if you might know anything about it. Look." She turned it over. "See? It's got the name of this shop stamped on the sole."

"Does it, now?" the man said, and Clara could see he was interested. Pulling his glasses down so that his hair flopped forward, he examined the sole of the shoe. He seemed to look at it for a long time. At last he straightened up.

"I'll have to get my ledger. We record the details of all the shoes we make," he said, disappearing behind a heavy velvet curtain.

"The music—it's *Swan Lake*," whispered Peter. "Pretend I'm von Rothbart!" He pirouetted fiercely across the shop floor, flapping his arms menacingly at Clara before turning away and gazing haughtily into the distance. Amelia-Ann applauded softly, and Peter lowered his arms just as the man reappeared bearing a pile of dusty-looking books and handed the shoe back to Clara.

"Could you read the number out to me, dear? My eyes aren't what they used to be," he said.

Clara picked up the shoe and squinted. The numbers really were very small.

"Zero-two-eight-six-five-eight," she said.

"Fifty-eight," the man repeated. "That tells us which year we made it in."

"Nineteen fifty-eight? That means it's sixteen years old! No wonder it looks ancient," said Amelia-Ann.

The man drew out a book nearer the bottom of the pile.

"Not that one, no, ah, it's this one." The books looked old, with dusty dark-green covers. Inside, the heavy cream paper was closely lined. The man flicked through page after page. "First four numbers, dear?" He peered at Clara. His glasses had slipped down his nose.

"Zero-two-eight-six," said Clara. The man, breathing heavily, pored over the lists lining the pages of the ledger, his finger tracing the numbers as he went. Clara wished he would hurry up. She felt as though she were on tenterhooks. At last his finger came to a stop.

"No, that can't be right." He glanced up. "Give me that," he said almost sharply, gesturing at the shoe that Clara was still holding. Silently, she handed it over. His manner had changed. He was peering closely at the numbers again. The children waited.

Once upon a time, that shoe held life, thought Clara. Someone had slipped their foot into it, and it had fitted them perfectly, like a second skin or a glove.

"How did you get it?" the man was asking, looking at both Clara and Peter properly for the first time, a frown etched on his features. "Come on, where did you find it?"

"At home," said Clara. "Why, what is it?" She felt a sudden unease.

The man lowered himself heavily onto the stool behind

the counter. "That shoe," he said, "belonged to a young dancer who was destined to be one of the greats." He rose from the stool again, anxiety giving way to bad temper. "Come on, children, you stole it, didn't you?"

"They did not!" said Amelia-Ann, rising indignantly from her stool.

"She's right—we didn't!" agreed Peter.

The old man sat down again and shook his head. "It was not to be," he muttered. "It was not to be." He rubbed his eyes and pushed his hair back again with the glasses.

"What was not to be?" asked Clara. Suddenly the forlorn ballet shoe seemed to be full of something. She wasn't sure what. Promise? Hope? Or was it fear? Clara felt a tremor of misgiving.

"Christobel Starling," cried the old man excitedly. "Dropped down dead, quite literally, in the middle of what most critics believe would have been the performance that made her name. She was on the cusp of stardom."

Clara went very still. Time seemed to stop.

"What performance?" whispered Peter.

"*Swan Lake*," said the old man. "The poor girl was in the middle of it and . . . *poof*—" He mimed blowing out a candle. "Gone. Quite gone."

THIRTEEN

CLARA FELT LIKE SHE HAD BEEN THUMPED HARD IN the chest.

The music had stopped playing. A potent silence filled the air.

"Christobel Starling was my mum," she managed to say. Peter's mouth, she noticed, had fixed itself into a shocked O. The palm tree of hair on top of Amelia-Ann's head had collapsed, as though it had been felled.

"Oh, my poor girl," the old man was saying. "I am so sorry. This is news to you, I see." He flapped his hands anxiously. "I didn't know she'd had a child." He lowered his glasses and peered at Clara again. "She must have been very young when you were born."

But Clara had stopped listening and was crashing

backward, away from the man, out of the shop and down the street. She felt strangely liquid, as though everything were dissolving. Her mother, Christobel Starling, had died giving birth to her! That was what she had always been told. If the man was telling the truth, then Uncle had lied. Why would he do that? And what if he'd lied about other things, too?"

This was so unexpected, so . . . big. Clara felt like her head might explode. The ballet shoe belonged to her mother. Her mother had been a ballerina. Clara would have been a baby when her mother died.

"Clara! Wait!" Peter and Amelia-Ann were chasing after her. She stopped. Her head felt like it was full of the heaviest matter, pressing down on her skull and temples, squeezing so much it hurt. She had the curious sensation that she was crying *behind* her eyes, hot, burning tears with nowhere to go.

"Clara." Peter's hand was on her shoulder. She turned, expecting to see her confusion mirrored in his face, but Peter's eyes were bright. "I can't believe it! You're so lucky! Imagine, your mum, a famous ballet dancer!"

Now Peter was pirouetting in the street. Amelia-Ann stood quietly, her button eyes anxious, darting from Peter to Clara.

"Christobel Starling, what a glamorous name," he continued. He made an elaborate curtsy, gesturing thanks to an imaginary audience, accepting applause and catching bouquets of flowers.

"Stop!" Clara said, and then she immediately wished she hadn't when Peter's smile faltered and he halted mid-curtsy, embarrassment flashing across his face.

And then the tears did fight their way out of her eyes, and her legs went all wobbly, so she had to sit down on the curb, even though there were cigarette butts everywhere. Peter sat down on one side, patting her on the shoulder, and Amelia-Ann sat on the other, holding her hand.

"I know you love ballet and everything, Peter," she said between big hiccupy sobs. "But so what if she was the most famous, the most beautiful, the most marvelous ballet dancer in all the world? The important thing is: Why would Uncle tell me she died when I was born instead of when she was dancing some stupid ballet?"

"*Swan Lake* is not a stupid ballet, Clara. It's one of the most—"

"All this time I thought she died *because of me*," Clara interrupted. It was the first time she had properly admitted it to herself, let alone anyone else. It had been a stubborn, scary, uncomfortable thought buried away in the furthermost corner of her heart, like a sharp stone, impossible to dislodge.

When Clara's sobs had turned to shuddery sighs, Peter asked if she had any of Uncle's cash with her.

Clara nodded. She had tucked it into her sock.

"He left you two hundred pounds?" exclaimed Amelia-Ann. "If I'd known that, I would've asked you to buy the nail polish for me!"

Clara smiled weakly. "And if I'd known you wanted it, I would have offered to get it for you!"

"Let's go and have a first-rate breakfast," said Peter. "That's what Granny and I always do after we've had a shock."

So they went into the Brass Kettle, and even though it was four in the afternoon and way past breakfast time, Clara had a full English breakfast (fried egg, bacon, sausage, beans, toast, black pudding, and mushrooms), Amelia-Ann had smoked kippers, and Peter had egg, fries, tomatoes, and extra-white sliced bread. Even Stockwell was allowed some scrambled eggs.

"What shocks did you and Granny actually have?" asked Clara, biting into a crisp slice of toast dipped in egg yolk. She was starting to feel better already.

"Oh, loads!" said Peter, taking a slurp of tea. "Once, a

pigeon flew in the window and pooped all over the furniture, and it took forever to chase it out. Another time a boy on a bike tried to grab Granny's bag, but she held on to it and whacked him over the head."

"Then what happened?" asked Clara. There was something so chirpy about Peter. In fact, he had been getting steadily chirpier since the day they met. Here he was with his granny ill and all his worries about the rent and stuff, and yet he hadn't complained in a long time. She'd been so caught up in her own worries about Braithwaite Manor, and then throwing herself into her newfound friendship with Amelia-Ann and Luci and Curtis, that she hadn't thought to ask if he was OK. She must remember to look after him, just as he was looking after her.

"He ran away," said Peter proudly. "Then there was the time when the frying pan caught fire. We had to call the fire department and everything . . ."

"Did your apartment burn down?" asked Amelia-Ann.

"No, thank goodness," said Peter. "The firemen put it out. Shocks are two-a-penny around our way."

Clara watched as Peter stirred a few more heaped spoons of sugar into his tea.

"I'm sure your granny will get well soon," she said. Peter looked up, surprised, and for a minute his eyes glistened.

"She's better," he said, taking a very long slurp of his tea.

"Look," Clara said urgently, "I need to do something—find out what's true and what's not." She had thought her past was a dead end, but it wasn't. She had found a tantalizing thread that needed following. And whereas Peter had made it plain that he didn't want to know about his own beginnings, she *did* want to know about hers. Desperately.

"Maybe there are more secrets to find out," said Amelia-Ann.

Peter set his mug down and furrowed his brow. It wasn't his sad pug frown though, it was his thinking frown. "Did your uncle never say a word about her?" he asked. "What about a photograph? You must've seen a picture of her."

"No!" said Clara. "Uncle forbade any mention of her. And the only pictures we had were those old paintings of the ancestors. There was nothing modern—and nothing of her."

"Well, we'd better fix that," said Peter purposefully. "It shouldn't be hard to find out more about Christobel if she really was *on the cusp* like the man said."

"What *is* on the cusp?" asked Amelia-Ann.

"Sort of . . . a turning point," explained Clara.

"Like she was about to be really well-known," added Peter helpfully.

"If *I* had a sister who was an almost famous ballet

dancer, I'd be really proud," said Amelia-Ann. "I wouldn't cover it up and forbid anyone to talk about it."

She was right, thought Clara. Why would anyone do that? There had to be a reason, and she was determined to find out.

"But where shall we start?" she said.

"Well . . ." said Peter, and Clara watched as a thought dawned on him and the idea spread across his features and transformed his face. "I know!" He slapped his forehead with his hand. "Last year our class went on a trip to the Colindale newspaper library, at the end of the Northern Line. They keep all the old newspapers there. We researched all these famous people by looking at their obituaries in the *Guardian*. There's bound to be something about Christobel Starling in there. We can go and read everything they've got, Clara!"

A small bud of excitement started to unfurl in Clara's chest. It would be a proper adventure.

"We can go on the train," continued Peter, "if you can pay for my fare."

"Of course I'll pay," said Clara, little starbursts exploding inside her. "It's my mum we're finding out about, after all. Let's go tomorrow. And," she added, "we can visit your gran!"

Peter was grinning, thrilled at the idea of London and his gran, but Amelia-Ann sighed into her teacup. "If only I could come, too," she said wistfully.

"You can. I've got enough money for all of us," said Clara, waving some of the ten-pound notes under Amelia-Ann's nose.

"I can't," said Amelia-Ann glumly. "Nan would have a heart attack. You'd better promise you'll come back and tell me what you find out."

"Cross our hearts and hope to die!" said Clara. It was something she had heard the others say. Of course she would come back. Wild horses couldn't keep her away!

FOURTEEN

THEY MANAGED TO MEET TOM AT THE ALLOTTED
time and drove back across the moors to Braithwaite
Manor. As they approached the house, Clara, who had been
dozing, sat up with a jolt. That was odd. All the lights were
blazing. Even odder, a silhouetted figure stood waiting for
them at the front door.

In an instant, Clara's mood plummeted. Someone had
found out about her. They'd come from the authorities, and
they were going to take her away. A huge lump of disappointment wedged itself in her throat.

But as Clara slumped, Peter scrabbled to get out of
the car, and then he was running like mad toward the
figure and the house. "Is Granny all right?" he yelled.
Clara clambered out after him. She had glimpsed his face

before he had darted off, shocked and white. Something was wrong.

"What is it? Is she OK?" His voice sounded reed-thin and panicky.

"Peter, darling." The speaker was a woman, Clara saw. "She's fine. You *know* I wouldn't have left her if she wasn't. The Framlinghams are looking out for her."

Clara stood behind Peter. She had never seen anyone so . . . distinctive. The woman was exceptionally elegant: tall and willowy. She had the most extraordinary toffee-colored hair, coiled into a bun at the nape of her neck. Her green eyes were flecked with amber, and her mouth was painted a perfect mailbox red.

"Then why are you here?" asked Peter.

"I *knew* something was wrong," the woman said, flicking a long, diaphanous scarf over her shoulder. She had a low musical voice and expressive hands that danced about as she talked. "I kept phoning and phoning, but the line was dead. Forgive me," she said, turning Clara. "I'm being rude. I'm Stella Jones. Peter has probably told you about me. You must be Clara." It was a statement, rather than a question, as though Stella was used to being right.

Clara nodded. When Peter had told her about Stella, she hadn't imagined she would look like this. The woman smelled delicious. It was a vivid, heady scent, like exotic flowers after heavy rain.

"Darling, where *is* your uncle?" No one had ever called Clara *darling* before. Sometimes Cook called her *dear* or *ducks*. *Darling* was miles better.

For a minute, Clara was quiet. She had known the question was coming, and now here it was, on a plate. Was this the end? What would Stella Jones think about her fending for herself, all alone? Stella's green eyes were on her, waiting for an answer. And Peter was waiting, too. He wasn't mouthing anything at her; his eyes weren't telling her what to say.

"Uncle's gone," she said truthfully. "We don't know where to."

༄

Stella had managed to get the electricity back on and had brought mountains of provisions with her in a capacious crocodile-skin bag. It was all food that Clara had never tasted before: crispy pancakes stuffed with chicken and sweet corn, Chinese food that you boiled in a bag, pizza with chunks of pineapple on top.

"Why didn't you call and tell me Edward wasn't here?" Stella asked as they sat down to a feast of chicken chow mein, shrimp balls, and sticky fried rice.

"We didn't want to worry Granny," said Peter. "And

it wouldn't have made any difference if he *were* here. He always used to ignore you, didn't he, Clara?"

Clara dipped a shrimp ball in bright-orange sauce and licked it off. It would have made quite a difference, actually. She didn't think Peter had grasped quite how dreadful Uncle's rules and routine had been.

"Peter, whether that's true or not, I promised Elsa I would look after you," said Stella firmly. "That's why I'm here. Your granny would never forgive me if something happened to you."

"How long are you staying?" asked Peter.

"I think another week, then she'll be well enough for us both to go back."

"Have social services been around?"

He still sounded anxious, thought Clara.

"I spoke to them on the phone. I think we can keep them at bay if we play our cards right."

Clara hardly dared ask what that plan would mean for her.

"Clara," Stella said, as if she could read her mind, "we need to find out what has happened to your uncle. You do know, don't you, that you can't stay here on your own?"

"But we've been fine so far, haven't we, Peter?" protested Clara.

"I'm sure you have, and if it were up to me, I'd let you get on with it. Alas"—Stella regarded them both seriously—"the rest of the world would not agree. I'm sure Edward will be back soon."

I hope not, Clara thought. *From the bottom of my heart.*

"Could Clara come home with us next week, then?" asked Peter.

"We'll see," said Stella, expertly rearranging her scarf and standing up. "In the meantime, Edward's study looks like a hurricane has hit it. While I'm here, I'm going to sort it out."

"So we can't sleep in there anymore?" asked Clara. It wasn't fair. They'd been managing perfectly well. And they'd made it so cozy!

"No," said Stella decisively. "You can do whatever you like in the rest of the house, but the study is out of bounds from now on."

Clara looked at Peter to see if he was going to object, but he was nodding in agreement. She decided she had better go along with it for now. After all, one rule wasn't so bad compared to the millions she'd endured before.

In fact, it turned out that their new hideout was even better than the old one. That evening they carted all their stuff up to the turret. They lugged up several quilts and cushions and piled them high to make a soft, downy bed. They carried up a nest of tables on which they placed candles from James's stores, so that the light was just as flickery as it had been in the study. To this arrangement they added the ballet shoe, Clara's books, and her shell box. It was warm and snug, like a gentleman's study, a cozy place to think important thoughts. Once everything was done, they sat down for a talk.

Clara was adamant that they should stick to their plan and leave for Colindale the following morning, but Peter was equally adamant that they should wait.

"If we go now, Stella will think we've run away," he protested. "She'll tell the police, and it'll ruin everything." The authorities would be notified, and Clara might be put away in a home. Social services would definitely split him and Granny up.

Clara felt a pang. Since Uncle had left and Peter had arrived, she had experienced such glorious freedom; she couldn't imagine it being taken away. Because Peter had seemed to shrug off his worries, she had assumed he felt the same way, too. But now it struck her that Peter already had his "something better," and it was his granny and their apartment.

More than anything, she wanted to go on with their

adventure, find out more about her mother and why Uncle had kept such a big secret. But she also knew she couldn't jeopardize things for Peter and his granny. She would wait. And when Stella and Peter went to London next week, somehow she would go, too.

～

The next day, Stella didn't bother them at all. They could play out on the moor as long as they liked, bound up the stairs and slide down the banisters to their hearts' content. She never came out of the study and told them to be quiet.

She had brought LPs with her from London, and a portable record player, and when she lowered the needle onto the smooth vinyl, the sound blasted all over the house. It was swirling, hypnotic music that made Peter grin and dance. He taught Clara how to do an arabesque and fast, furious pirouettes; he practiced a cabriole, which was a kind of leap through the air. He was miles more graceful than Clara and made her feel like a clodhopper. And yet, however clumsy she was, the dancing and the music made her feel closer to her mother. Is this what Christobel had felt like, wild and free when she danced? Had she practiced here, in this very room?

In the afternoon, Amelia-Ann trotted over on Dapple. She had glimpsed Stella Jones from the car and was desperate to know more. In Stella's bedroom they sifted through her jewelry, trying different pieces on. Clara loved the choker with the silver snake clasp, and Peter, the jangly bracelets that you could push all the way up to the top of your arms. They painted their faces with her make-up and paraded around in her long floaty scarves. Clara was surprised Stella didn't sweep in and tell them not to touch her stuff. But it seemed she had meant what she said: the children could have the run of the house while she brought order to the study.

FIFTEEN

$\mathcal{A}$FTER TWO DAYS OF LEAVING THE CHILDREN TO their own devices, Stella arrived at the breakfast table in a whirl of scarves and perfume. She had telephoned for a taxi. They were going to Leeds for the day.

"I have to go to the bank," she said, "and do some shopping. You can find something to do while I'm busy, can't you?"

By the time the taxi dropped them off, Peter and Clara had decided they would spend the day at the library. If they couldn't go to the Colindale newspaper library, they would start their research in Leeds. Stella gave them lunch money and told them she would meet them by the library steps at four p.m.

The library was enormous, light and airy, with separate

floors for adults and children. Clara gazed around in wonder. It was as if she had been catapulted into a treasure trove. There were probably enough books here, she thought, to read until she grew old and died.

Downstairs in the adult library, the information books were ordered by number. Peter led the way to the 700s, where there were three whole shelves groaning with ballet-related books. "Yes!" said Peter, punching the air with his fist. He had read every single ballet book in his library several times over, and now here were a whole load more. They set up base camp and then carted over piles of books at a time, lounging on the carpet and leafing through them, eyes alert for any mention of Clara's mother. There were books about choreographers, and the history of ballet, and books full of ballet stories. There was a *Who's Who in Ballet*, but as Peter pointed out, it was ancient, published in 1950, so that was no good. There were tons of books about Nureyev, one of which Peter hid in his bag. But they couldn't find anything about Christobel Starling.

"I think it's because she was *on the cusp*." Clara sighed. "No one had a chance to put her in a book before she died."

Swallowing her disappointment, she listened while Peter read aloud to her. He was particularly pleased when he discovered that Nureyev, because he was so poor, hadn't started ballet school until he was seventeen, when everyone else had been going since they were nine.

"There's hope for you yet, then," said Clara, only half joking. Then she made Peter take the book out of his bag to borrow like a normal person, and they went up to the counter.

"No school today?" asked the librarian.

"No," said Peter. "The heating broke down so they sent us home." Clara gave him an admiring sideways glance for his quick thinking.

"Got your library card?"

"Ummm ..." said Clara.

"I've left mine at home, and she doesn't have one," said Peter. "Can she join?"

"Of course." The librarian reached for a form and passed it to Clara. "You just need to fill this out," she said. "And you need to get your mum or dad to sign it."

"She hasn't got a mum or dad," said Peter quickly. Clara darted a glance at him, and he gave her the tiniest of winks. He was playing a game!

She tried to look forlorn.

"They died last year in a car crash," she said. Her hand went to her eyes as if to wipe away a tear.

"Oh, my dear," said the librarian, looking at Clara with

113

concern. "But . . . who's looking after you—foster parents? Children's home?"

"I *was* with a foster family," said Clara, enjoying herself now, "but they were horrible! I had to sleep in the laundry cupboard, and at mealtimes I wasn't allowed to sit with the family. I had to eat mine in the pantry. And the other children, their children, were so cruel! They tried to cut my braids off when I was asleep!"

"She's being moved to a different family today," said Peter very solemnly. He looked at Clara sympathetically. "You could ask them to sign it . . . ?"

"No, no, don't worry," the librarian said hurriedly. "I'll write you a temporary ticket for now. You can take the book today, my pet, and get the form signed when you're settled."

"Oh, thank you," said Clara gratefully. As the librarian bent her head to write the ticket, Peter winked at Clara and gave her a thumbs-up. Clara gave him a thumbs-up back. She felt a bit more cheerful even though they hadn't made any headway in their research. They were a team, she thought. Kindred spirits, even.

"OK, there you are." The librarian passed Clara the stamped book. "And now I'm afraid it's time to go. We close at lunchtime on Thursdays. On your way out, take a look at the bulletin board. There's a poster there that might interest you."

Taking the book, they raced to the lobby, and sure enough, there on the bulletin board was a fiery yellow-and-red poster with dancers leaping across it. A ballerina with cat's eyes held a perfect arabesque. A man in glittery turquoise plumes soared behind her like an exotic bird. KIROV BALLET! it declared. LONDON, LEEDS, EDINBURGH. FIRST TOUR IN **TWELVE** YEARS!

"Remember I told you that Nureyev used to dance with the Kirov before he defected?" said Peter, leaping dramatically across the lobby in a fairly good imitation of the man in the turquoise plumes. "Maybe he'll go to see them, for old times' sake!"

∾

Outside, the wind was freezing, biting at them with icy shark's teeth. They bought fish and chips from The Cod Father, doused them with so much vinegar it made their eyes water, and ate them, hot and salty, straight out of the newspaper wrapping.

"I'm f-f-freeeezing, Clara," said Peter as he crumpled up his empty wrapper and tossed it in the trash. "What are we going to do all afternoon now that the library's closed?"

"We could go browsing in one of the department stores,"

suggested Clara. She wasn't sure if it would be as much fun without Amelia-Ann, but at least it would be warm and dry.

But when they got to the shops, most of them were closed, too. It appeared that it was early-closing day all over Leeds.

"Look!" cried Peter.

A flurry of snowflakes danced in the air. Clara held out her hand to catch them.

"Snow," she said, puzzled. "Don't you get snow in London?"

"What? Yes! Well, not very much. But I don't mean the snow. Look!"

Clara looked. All she could see were cars and buses and people.

"It's Stella! She just went around that corner," Peter said. "Let's catch up with her and tell her we've been kicked out of the library."

But by the time they had crossed the road and rounded the corner, Stella was nowhere to be seen. They scanned the street, looking for her toffee-colored hair, her camel coat with the fur collar, and the patent leather shoes with curved heels and straps at the ankles that winked as she walked.

"Let's try this way," Clara said. They walked to the end of

the road, looked right, looked left. "There!" Clara pointed. She caught a glimpse of Stella making a sharp turn and then tip-tapping up the steps of a grand hotel.

"What's she going in there for?" asked Peter. "I thought she was going to the bank!"

The hotel Stella had disappeared into was called the Metropole, and it was dazzling: huge and stately with a wide staircase sweeping up to an imposing entrance. Outside, uniformed doormen stood at attention; people stepped out of sleek-looking cars that purred up to deposit them; through elegantly arched windows, chandeliers glimmered and luxury beckoned. Clara started to swish up the steps.

"Wait!" Peter tugged Clara back. "We can't just walk in there! I *know* about posh hotels." Granny, it turned out, had once been a cleaner at Claridge's.

Clara didn't have an inkling what Claridge's was.

"You haven't heard of Claridge's?" Peter exclaimed. "What about the Ritz? The Savoy?" He rattled off a list of the poshest of posh hotels.

Clara hadn't heard of any of them.

"The Queen Mother has lunch at Claridge's! And once Granny saw Jackie O!"

Clara couldn't care less about the Queen Mother and

she didn't have a clue who Jackie O was. All she wanted to do was swish up the steps. They were the kind of steps that were just made for swishing, and if Stella could, why couldn't she?

"It *is* a bit odd," said Peter. "I wonder what she's up to? I think we should spy. Come on!"

Clara followed Peter around the back of the hotel to an entrance that looked nothing like the one at the front: a small, unmarked door on a narrow, shabby street. A young man in a chef's hat and apron stood outside taking long puffs on a cigarette.

"Now then, laddie, what you up to?" he asked as Peter squeezed past to open the door.

"Going to see my mum," said Peter, normal as could be. "She cleans on Thursdays. She forgot her purse and stuff—I'm bringing them to her."

"Doris, is it?" said the smoking chef, and not missing a beat, Peter nodded.

"Right y'are, then. Any friend of the lovely Doris is a friend of mine. Go on in." And he held the door open so Clara could follow.

The rear of the hotel was worlds away from the scene Clara had glimpsed from the front. Everything was painted a sort of dreary green, the strip lighting casting an unforgiving glare on the maze of corridors and passage-ways that they hurried along.

"Peter, wait! I don't think Stella's going to come back here, do you?"

"Of course she won't come back here," Peter called over his shoulder. "But it's the only way we'll get to the front of the hotel without being stopped by the doormen and whatnot."

And he was right. No one gave them a passing glance as they made their way through the laundry rooms—washing machines thrumming comfortingly, the air heavy and warm and detergenty—and then skirted around the kitchens, chaotic with clatter and steam. Passing ranks of harried-looking sous-chefs and flustered kitchen staff, they pushed their way through a swinging door, and suddenly, there they were, in the hotel lobby where everything was shiny and gleaming, and in the distance a piano was tinkling.

Before anyone could spot them, Clara darted behind an enormous potted palm and pulled Peter in after her. The green fronds crackled and tickled her nose, but they also provided a convenient screen. It was the perfect spying place. She parted the leaves gently and peered through them. From where they were positioned, they had a direct view into the lounge.

Clara couldn't help but sigh at the utter beauty of it. The lounge was spacious, with pale-green silk walls and a thick cream carpet. There were plush green-velvet armchairs, the color of moss, and plump cushions scattered with embroidered flowers. A large table was neatly arranged with newspapers and magazines, and on smaller tables sat silver bowls of the palest pink roses. In the far corner of the room was the piano they had heard, a glossy-black baby grand; if she craned her neck, Clara could just about glimpse the upright back of the pianist.

It was evidently a quiet time of day, not long after lunch and still too early for supper, because only a handful of people were in there. Closest to them was a bony woman with an extraordinarily long neck. She wore gold-rimmed spectacles and was pecking unenthusiastically at what looked like a slice of Victoria sponge cake. Beyond her, a large couple with red faces argued quietly, eyes indignant, pinching each other to emphasize their points; in the farthest corner, near the piano, a man with a thatch of white-blond hair and black-framed glasses lay back on an elegant sofa, ankles crossed, eyes shut. He appeared to be asleep.

"Move over; I can't see," said Peter, gently elbowing Clara aside and sticking his head in front of hers. "Spitting image of Andy Warhol," he announced.

"Andy who?" whispered Clara.

"Famous artist," said Peter. "Paints cans of tomato soup and stuff. Look! There's Stella."

"What's she doing?" asked Clara. "Shall we jump out and surprise her?" She imagined Stella's look of shock and then all of them falling down laughing.

"Not here, we'll get in trouble," he whispered. "Look, she's going over to Andy Warhol! She's sitting down with him. Look! He's awake now. They're arguing about something!"

Peter stretched even farther into the palm leaves to get a better look. "Actually," he said, "the real Andy Warhol looks kind of weird. This man's much more handsome. Maybe he's Stella's secret lover!"

Clara dug Peter in the ribs. "Budge out of the way, I can't see a thing."

Peter drew back, and Clara took his place. The leaves made her want to sneeze. There, beyond the bony woman and the red-faced couple, was Stella and the man with the white hair. Were they arguing? The man was scowling, and a familiar muscle twitched under his right eye. Clara went cold.

"That," she said, "is Uncle. And he's dyed his hair."

SIXTEEN

EVEN THOUGH THEY RAN ALL THE WAY BACK, Clara and Peter only managed to get to the library steps a mere five minutes before Stella.

"Act normal," said Peter, who had his hands in his pockets and was absentmindedly kicking the steps. He gave a good impression of someone who didn't have a care in the world. But Clara felt hot and prickly, her thoughts a spiky set of questions stabbing around in her head. What was Uncle doing at the Metropole? Why had he dyed his hair? Anyone would think *he* was some kind of spy—or a criminal on the run. Which, come to think of it, he probably was. He had, after all, abandoned her in the village, even if he had expected her to throw herself on the mercy of Cook.

As soon as Stella was within hearing distance, Clara burst out, "Did you find Uncle?"

"What? No, darling," said Stella, looking surprised. "I told you, I came for the bank, not to find your uncle. Goodness knows where he has gone."

A little gasp escaped Clara's lips at Stella's outright lie, but Peter shot her a warning look, so she turned it into a cough.

"Darling? Are you all right? Why the white face? It's too cold. You should have waited for me in the library."

"But—" Clara started to speak, but Peter pinched her and she stopped.

"Library's closed," he said. "Got kicked out early."

"No wonder you look so pale. We need to go home and warm you up. Taxi!" Stella waved her arm to hail an approaching cab.

The taxi journey was agony. Clara could barely look at Peter; she was convinced his eyes would be enormous with the questions that were surely reflected in her own. But Peter kept up a constant stream of chatter about this and that and nothing in particular, and Clara understood that he was filling the journey with words so that there was no space for her questions.

Why had Stella lied? Maybe she was arranging for Uncle

to come back home, complete with all the dreaded rules and routines. She'd practically said that children couldn't live on their own. Perhaps she thought she was doing it for Clara's own good!

No, please, no, Clara thought.

When at last the taxi pulled up in front of Braithwaite Manor, she grabbed Peter by the hand and they raced into the house.

"Where are you going? I was about to start supper," called Stella.

"Up to the turret," Peter called back. "We'll be down in a bit."

They ran up the spiraling steps, taking two at a time. At the top they found Stockwell curled up in a ball on the mound of quilts, quietly oblivious to the drama at hand. "*What* is going on?" cried Clara, flopping down next to the cat.

"She must be hiding something," Peter said.

"Perhaps that's why she's always in Uncle's study," Clara said. She thought about the hours they had spent in Stella's bedroom trying on all her things and the noise they had made as they clattered around the house. "She let us do whatever we wanted as long as we didn't disturb her. What do you think she was doing in there?"

It must have been something she didn't want Clara to see. Maybe, a tentative thought started to crystallize in Clara's mind, that *something* had to do with her mother's past and why Uncle had "disappeared."

"We need to get in there . . ." she said slowly. "But first we need to get Stella out of the way."

"We'll have to distract her somehow." Peter screwed his face up tight, thinking.

"I've got an idea," said Clara. "But we'll need Amelia-Ann. She said she would come around after supper. We can ask her then."

∼

The next afternoon, Peter and Clara hung around in the garden shivering, waiting for the first part of their plan to spring into action. Stella, as usual, had been in the study all day.

"Where is Amelia-Ann?" Clara shivered. It was so cold it almost hurt to talk. They had been waiting a long time. Clara's teeth were chattering, and her frozen fingers felt like they were about to drop off and die. Peter's nose glowed pink. A nervous current ran between them. What if the plan didn't work?

At last Amelia-Ann arrived, running across the moor, hair flying, cheeks flushed.

"Where's Stella?" she shouted as she approached. "Stella! Get Stella!"

"What's the matter?" Stella was already at the door looking annoyed.

But Amelia-Ann waved her words away, her voice high and urgent.

"Nan says come quick . . . Mr. Starling, her uncle"—she pointed a trembling finger at Clara—"has arrived. He's raving like a loon about you and Clara and . . ."

"Uncle is at Cook's?" Clara shrieked, clutching her heart and looking agonized. She sensed Peter was looking at her, thinking she was going over the top, but she didn't care. This was fun.

And the plan *was* working. Stella's pale face had gone ashen, and now she had put a hand up, as if to ward off the words tumbling out of Amelia-Ann's mouth.

"Peter, Clara." She turned to them abruptly and there were two little pink spots high on her cheeks. Her mouth opened, then closed again. She seemed to be struggling to find the right words. "I'd better go and find out what's happening," she finally managed. "Stay here. I will be back."

And then she was actually running, fast, across the moor, no hat, no coat, and Amelia-Ann was clutching

Clara and saying in a rush, "I'll come back tonight, see how it went." And then she was gone, racing away after Stella. Toward the village.

Clara burst out laughing. Great gusts blew through her, tears streamed down her face. "Quick!" She hugged Peter with relief. "To the study. We haven't got long!"

SEVENTEEN

As far as Clara was concerned, the one redeeming thing about the study had always been the fireplace. No matter how chilly Uncle had been, the fire could always be relied on to burn brightly.

But no fire burned in the grate today, and the room looked stark and uninviting. It was as if a giant brush had swept the whole place clean. In the cold light of day, the leather armchairs looked stiff and uncomfortable, the curtains and rugs revealed as threadbare. No longer were towers of paper teetering on every surface, nor were letters and bills and books littering the floor.

"Wow," said Peter, "she *has* been busy."

The books were in the bookcase and had all been lined up in order by size and color. The scattered papers had been neatly sorted into the metal filing cabinet by the door. The bureau had been tidied, with letters tucked into one drawer and bills in the other. The desk had been scrubbed clean; not one ink spot remained. The collection of fountain pens had disappeared, and in their place was a solitary plastic ballpoint. Green.

They had to search and be quick about it. It wouldn't be long before Stella returned.

"I'll start with the letters. You look at the bills," declared Peter. So Clara began leafing through them, page after page filled with squiggly numbers that made no sense, covered in Uncle's scrawl, sums and workings-out filling the margins and sometimes fervently spilling out to cover the page. Among it all she found receipts for many of the things that had disappeared. A thousand pounds for a watercolor; fifty pounds for the paintings of farmyard animals that had decorated the hall; five hundred pounds for the blue-and-white soup tureen.

"Look." She showed Peter.

"Five hundred for a bowl?" he exclaimed. "That's our rent for five months!"

"Anything in the letters?"

"Yes," said Peter, "heaps of stuff about deeds and what-not. It all has to do with selling the house. Oh no! Clara, you're not going to like this. This one says, 'acting on behalf of Mr. and Mrs. Morden' and it's going on about 'converting the premises.' What does that mean?"

"But we put a stop to all that!" cried Clara. Anxiety plucked at her. The euphoria she had felt when Stella had fallen for their plan had vanished. Feverishly she opened the filing cabinet, which was also packed with correspondence.

"Quick," said Peter, who had finished going through his drawer and had come over to help her. "Just leaf through, see if anything stands out . . . There! Look, that one!" The address was written in green ink.

Clara pulled out the envelope Peter was referring to and drew out the thin paper from within. It crackled between her fingertips. The spiky message looked as though it had been hastily scrawled.

Eddie,
 Peter arriving on Saturday. He can be difficult. Hope everything is going to plan.
 S.

Eddie! Is that what other people called Uncle? It sounded like someone rakish, someone fun. The kind of person who would drop everything when the sun shone and take the convertible out for a spin. The kind of person who thought it was OK to eat cheese on toast while reading in bed or who slid down the banister instead of taking the stairs. It didn't seem like it could belong to coldhearted Uncle, Mr. *Edward* Starling.

"*S.* must be Stella," said Clara. "So he *did* know you were coming. And he still ran off!"

Peter's face had turned beet red. "I'm not difficult!" he said. "I only got into a few fights—that weren't even my fault!"

"She was probably just saying it because she was worried about you," soothed Clara. "And when she first suggested you come here, what did you say?"

"I s'pose I argued," admitted Peter, "but only 'cause I was worried about leaving Granny."

"Well, then," said Clara. "But what's all that about everything going to plan?"

"Dunno," said Peter, cracking his knuckles. "Maybe it's to do with sorting out his debts."

The door creaked open, and they both jumped. But it was only Stockwell coming to see what was going on.

Clara left Peter with the letters and went over to the bookcase. Her gaze roamed over the spines. Mainly novels: *The Woman in White, Bleak House* . . . But one book caught her eye. *A Guardian's Guide to Child Rearing.* That's what Uncle had been. Her guardian.

Pulling the book off the shelf, she opened it at random.

"'A regimental routine should not be underestimated,'" she read. "'See your ward no more than once a day. Inquire about their lessons and make sure they are being diligent in their prayers. Never show affection, it weakens the soul.'"

Clara hurled the book to the floor. "I hate Uncle," she blurted out.

"What's that?" asked Peter.

"What?"

"That . . ." Peter crouched down to retrieve a folded piece of paper that had slipped from the pages of the book.

Clara pounced and grabbed it from Peter. It was an old newspaper clipping, furrowed and creased where it had been folded for so long.

"Let's see," said Peter. Clara smoothed the paper out on the desk. The black-and-white photograph was grainy, but you could just about make out two people, arms linked, laughing. The young woman, who had pale curls, was gazing up at the man next to her. The man's head dipped down, his hair flopping across his features, but even so, you could tell he was looking straight into the woman's eyes.

Underneath the picture was a caption.

"'Springtime in Paris: out on the town with ballet's rising young stars,'" read Clara. "'Christobel Starling, and her beau'—I can't read the last name, it's on the crease and the print's all smudgy. Then it says, 'The new Nureyev?' with a question mark."

Clara touched the face of the curly-haired woman gently with her index finger. She couldn't believe she was finally looking at the only picture she had ever seen of her mother. "So it's true; she really was a ballerina!" she said, thrusting the newspaper clipping at Peter and then just as quickly grabbing it back. "That's my mum!"

She felt electric, her whole body buzzing like a live wire. She wished she could see Christobel Starling from every angle. What did she look like from the front, the back, the other side? She wanted to see her name written down. She wanted to absorb every part of her.

Now Clara and Peter pulled the books off the shelves, holding them upside down by the spines and shaking them to see if any more papers fluttered out.

"Good thing that librarian can't see us," muttered Peter as they dropped book after book on the floor, until finally they were rewarded with another photograph. A proper one this time.

"WHAT do you think you're doing? I told you the study was out of bounds."

Clara almost screamed. She tucked the photograph up her sleeve.

Neither of them had heard Stella come in. Strands of hair had escaped from her bun and spiked furiously around her face. Her usually pale complexion was flushed, and she was a little out of breath. Now she smoothed her hair down and glanced around the room, her eyes taking in the books that they had dropped on the floor.

"What on earth . . . ? Are you looking for something?"

"You met Uncle!" Clara couldn't hold it in any longer. "We saw you at the hotel; we followed you."

For a split second, surprise registered in Stella's eyes. Then she held up her hands. "Guilty as charged!" she said. "Sit down, Clara."

But Clara didn't want to sit down. She stared defiantly back at Stella and stayed resolutely on her feet.

"You both know that Edward is a good friend of mine, and I care for him deeply."

Clara snorted. How could anyone care for Uncle? He was the most uncareable-for person she knew.

"Yes, Clara, even though he wasn't the best guardian in the world"—Stella's eyes flicked over to the discarded *A Guardian's Guide to Child Rearing*—"he *is* still a human being, you know."

Clara didn't reply to that. She didn't know how.

"I did meet him, and I suppose I should have told you in

the first place. He's in terrible trouble. Debts up to his ears. And I promised to help him, like any good friend would. If Peter were in trouble, you'd help him, wouldn't you?"

Clara gave a small nod.

"Is he on the run, then?" asked Peter. He had scooped up Stockwell, who was staring at Stella intently.

"I wouldn't put it quite like that," said Stella. "The important thing is, if we can't sort the debts, the house will have to be sold and your uncle declared bankrupt. If that were to happen, I can't promise what would happen to you." Her green-gold eyes locked on Clara's gray ones. The words were said kindly, but they sent a shiver all the way up Clara's spine.

"Now," said Stella, "I suggest you two take off while I tidy this mess up. And we'll have a good talk about it later. OK?"

"You shouldn't trust him, even if he is your friend," said Clara. "He's a liar!"

"Why on earth would you say that, darling?" Now Stella looked taken aback.

"Because he lied to me. Before you came, I found out—"

But Peter didn't let her finish. Instead he deposited Stockwell in her arms and pushed her out of the room. The cat's fur was warm and comforting. "Clara, let's go to the turret," he said.

∿

"D'you trust her?" Clara asked Peter as soon as they were out of earshot. "D'you think she's telling the truth?"

"I don't know," said Peter. "She's been good to Granny. And what she said about friends sticking together, she's right about that, too." He gave Clara's hand a little squeeze. He was saying he was her friend, Clara thought. She squeezed his hand back. But anxiety still nipped at her.

"I can't wait any longer, Peter," she said. "We need to go to London now." She thought about the young woman with the blond curls. A ballet dancer. Out on the town in Paris with her beau.

"I know," said Peter, looking at his watch. "Let's go tonight. Amelia-Ann said she was coming back later, didn't she? We'll go when she gets here. What's that, Clara?"

It was the photograph she had slipped up her sleeve. Now the corner of it was poking out from her cuff, and Stockwell was batting at it with her paw, rubbing her face against its sharp corner.

Clara pulled it out. It was an old photograph, a color one, but the color was watery, washed out. It showed two women standing in front of a fountain. One of them had pale curly hair. Christobel! Clara had the most curious melting sensation when she looked at her. With some effort, she tore her gaze away and turned her attention to the other woman, whose toffee-colored hair was drawn back from her face.

"Peter, look!" Clara knew that face.

Flipping the photograph over, she read the message. "'S and C, 1960.'"

Stella knew Christobel?

Peter took the photograph and examined it. "I s'pose if she's such good friends with your uncle, then she must have known his sister."

Clara could see Peter was trying to make sense of it. But it didn't make sense. Why wouldn't Stella have said something? Now Clara felt angry again, furious, in fact.

"That's two secrets she's kept from us." She almost spat the words out. "I'm going back down to ask."

But the door at the bottom of the turret was closed. And when Clara tried to open it, it wouldn't budge. "Stella!" she shouted, but Stella had put her music on too loud and it hammered through the keyhole, vibrating almost, drowning Clara's words out.

Clara rattled the door again. It must be jammed. Or Stella had locked it. Why would she do that? Were they prisoners? Unless . . . she turned to find Peter and Stockwell staring at her, their eyes wide.

"I think she's guessed we're going to run away!"

EIGHTEEN

THEY RAN BACK UP TO THE ROOM AT THE TOP OF
the turret, and Peter began frantically emptying his
pockets: a chestnut, a piece of string, two hard candies, a
red ribbon.

"Is that my red ribbon?" asked Clara. Had Peter taken it
from her shell box? She wondered why.

"It's nothing," said Peter, stuffing it back into his pocket.
He had found what he was looking for—the little flashlight
he had stolen from the department store in Leeds. He went
over to the window and opened it, then began clicking at
the tiny switch so that the light flicked on and off, on and
off, glowing weakly in the late dusk.

"But—" Clara began, and then stopped herself. He *had*
stolen it. She remembered the marbles he'd taken along

with the flashlight in the department store and the book he'd almost taken from the library. It must have been a habit of his. She wanted to grab the ribbon back and tell Peter it was her mother's, and he had no right, even if he was her friend who would stick by her through thick and thin.

"What are you doing?" Clara felt shaky.

"Sending a message," he said bluntly. He was leaning as far out the window as he could, the flashlight held aloft. "SOS. Three short flashes, three long, then three short again. It's the international distress signal."

Clara thought about Braithwaite Manor standing all alone, marooned almost, in the middle of the dark moor. No one around for miles and miles. Would anyone even see it?

"It's for Amelia-Ann," said Peter. "We said we'd meet her in the garden, didn't we? But now we're trapped up here. She'll see the light, and then she'll know."

Clara shivered. She was hungry *and* freezing. All they had to share between them were the two candies that Peter had in his pocket. Clara chose the green one. It was sweetly acidic and made her stomach growl even more. To keep warm, they wrapped themselves in the quilts. Clara felt like her stomach was full of jumping beans. Were they going to be stuck in here all night? She couldn't bear it! All she wanted to do was get out, get to London, and find out more about Christobel.

It must have been almost midnight when at last they heard the faint crunch of footsteps down below.

"Is that her?" Clara jumped up and peered out into the inky blackness. "Amelia-Ann," she said, but there was no answer. She grabbed Peter's flashlight and flicked it on and off, three short, three long, three short. Nothing. It was quite probable that Amelia-Ann didn't recognize the international distress signal either. They'd have to try something else. Quickly Clara shone the light around the room, looking for a scrap of paper. She grabbed *The Wolves of Willoughby Chase* and tore out the title page.

"We're trapped!" she wrote. "Help us so we can go to London!"

"Here, wrap it round this," said Peter, passing her the chestnut. "To weigh it down."

Clara wrapped the note around the chestnut and hurled it out the window.

Would Amelia-Ann see the note in the dark? They waited, straining to hear something, anything. But the only sound that floated through the narrow window was the low moan of the wind, and then . . . What was that?

More footsteps! But instead of getting louder, they were fading way.

"She's gone," said Clara, and a wave of disappointment washed over her. "She didn't see." But even if she had seen, Clara thought to herself, what could she have done?

It got later and later, but neither of them felt like sleeping. Clara's thoughts grew more and more tangled, a muddle of her mother, her uncle, Stella, the house, Mr. and Mrs. Morden, and Jackson Smith.

Then at last, just when they had both given up all hope, there came a long, low whistle.

"She's back!" said Peter, kicking off the quilt and rising to stick his head out the window.

Clara shoved her portion of the quilt aside and scrambled unsteadily to her feet. She was stiff with cold. Silently, Peter made space for her so she could see out.

It was not quite dawn and, at first, in the murky blue light, she couldn't make out a thing. She blinked and looked again, searching the shadows. There! Something loomed. Something tall and hulking. Clara rubbed her eyes with her knuckles. But there must be something wrong with them. She still couldn't see. She looked again, forcing herself to focus, be steady, hold her gaze. At last the shadows took shape. Rearing out of the gloom was Curtis, standing tall on

Dapple's back. And there was Amelia-Ann, standing next to the horse, waving silently. Relief surged through Clara. Help had come!

Amelia-Ann was holding something. Something coiled and heavy, dripping to the ground and trailing snakelike behind her. Clara watched her tie a loop in it and hand it to Curtis, who swirled it high above his head in big circles. He whipped it around and around in the air and then, *flash*, all of a sudden it shot up to the window where Clara stood. She tried to grab at it, but her fingers barely brushed the rough, raspy rope before it dropped, to land with a soft thud, puddled below.

Amelia-Ann's hands shot up, as if in despair. She passed the rope back to Curtis, and he tried again, around and around, faster and faster, and then it flew toward Clara, and Peter hissed, "Reach it, Clara! Reach it!" But she couldn't reach it—it wasn't long enough—and then, *thud*, it landed again in a mound on the ground.

"Why didn't you catch it?"

"I couldn't!" Clara snapped.

"Let me try next time," said Peter, attempting to elbow Clara out of the way.

"No," said Clara, shoving him back. "Your arms are shorter than mine."

"They are not!" Peter was indignant, but Clara ignored him. Below in the gloom, she could see Amelia-Ann bending down so that Luci could scramble onto her shoulders and onto the horse. Then Curtis bent his knees so he was crouching, and Luci climbed onto Curtis's shoulders, planting her feet firmly on either side of his neck. Curtis rose slowly, and as he did so, Luci straightened up and there they stood, proud and straight and tall like circus performers.

Now the rope was in Luci's hands and she swirled it above her head, whipping it around and around in a frenzy, and then *whoosh*, it shot straight at Clara and this time she caught it, clutching its roughness and pulling it in.

Barely perceptible, a whisper floated up from below. "Rapunzel, Rapunzel, let down your hair!"

"Genius!" Peter breathed out, helping Clara haul in the thick rope. "It's the braid Amelia-Ann told us about! The one her nan was knitting out of fishing nets!"

Peter went to tie the rope to the doorknob, but Clara stopped him.

"Not there," she said. "Up here." A metal rail stretched above the window where once, long ago, curtains would have hung. Quickly, Peter tied a knot.

"A bowline knot," he said, giving the rope a good

tug. "Granny gave me a book called *Knot Know-How* for my birthday."

"Will it be strong enough?" asked Clara. How far could you fall without breaking any bones?

"This is the king of knots," said Peter. "It'd hold the weight of an elephant. You go first."

Clara looked out the window and felt a sliver of fear. It was a long way down. But the alternative was to just stay here, waiting. She couldn't do that. She had to do something, make something happen, even if she risked breaking all her bones.

"Hand over hand," said Peter. "Keep your feet on the wall and go slowly."

It was a squeeze getting out because the window was so narrow, but Clara eased herself through it so that she was able to crouch on the window ledge and observe the rope dangling in a straight line below. Then she grabbed the coarse braid with both hands and launched herself into nothingness. There was a vibration as the rope took her full weight, and for a terrible moment Clara hung there, clinging on for dear life, her feet kicking uselessly, knowing that at any moment she might drop.

But she didn't. Miracle of miracles, the rope held, and then she was leaning back and using all her strength to push her feet against the wall, her legs rigid and her arms taut, and then her body was doing the work for her, and she started to get the hang of it: hand over hand, foot over foot.

Down she went, silently, stealthily, slithering and sliding, her hands burning like they were on fire. And then she was at the bottom, and Peter followed her, Stockwell's head poking out of the front of his sweater. In the early morning gloom, they ran on tiptoe down the drive. Clara saw that Dapple was wearing enormous knitted socks tied with string on her hooves, and she nearly laughed out loud. They had escaped! They were leaving Stella and Uncle and everything else behind. London beckoned, and maybe, just maybe, Clara thought, she would find some answers to her questions.

NINETEEN

THEY WENT TO COOK'S HOUSE FIRST BECAUSE IT was still too early for the train. "We've told Nan your uncle's disappeared, but it's OK because now you're going to stay with Peter's granny," Amelia-Ann warned as they entered the stone cottage.

"Ducks!" exclaimed Cook as the children swarmed into the kitchen. She was dressed in a red flannel robe and was standing at the stove minding a number of sizzling pans.

She gave Clara a warm hug. "I couldn't let you go off to London without a proper breakfast inside you, now, could I? Amelia-Ann, take everyone's coats. Luci and Curtis, set the table."

The house was warm and chaotic, full of noise and

chatter and something else . . . Clara wasn't sure what it was exactly, but if felt safe. Like being wrapped in cotton balls.

Breakfast was delicious: fried eggs, bacon, a sausage each, and grilled tomatoes.

"Amelia-Ann's told me everything," said Cook as she poured the tea. "I can't believe Mr. S. just up and left! Shocking it is, shocking. Why on earth you didn't just come straight here, I'll never know."

"It's been fine," Clara reassured her. "He left me money and I bought tea and cake and I found my own way home."

"Well, I can't say I'm surprised," said Cook, setting down extra toast and a jar of amber-colored marmalade. It looked much nicer than the stuff they had at Braithwaite Manor. "He was a terrible employer—you saw how he expected me to manage on that skimpy housekeeping budget. And," she added darkly, "I've been hearing all sorts of stories from the other villagers. Of him in his younger days."

"Like what?" asked Clara. She tried to picture Uncle in his younger days, but she couldn't; he was just one of those people who seemed eternally old.

"Well." Cook stopped bustling and sat down. "They say he was a bit of a wild one. Fell in with some disreputables, started gambling, ran up a whole lot of debts. Drove Lord and Lady Starling mad by all accounts. He was never meant to come back."

"Come back from where?" said Clara.

"When he was eighteen, they told him to leave."

Cook paused and blew on her tea to cool it down.

"Why? What did he do?"

"He owed a terrible amount of money," Cook said. "So he *stole* the family jewels and sold them to pay off his debts! Blamed the theft on the butler. The lord and lady were so furious when they found out that they changed their will and made Christobel the sole heir."

"Cook!" Clara exclaimed. "Why didn't you say anything about this before?"

"Village gossip. Only comes out in dribs and drabs," said Cook stoutly. "Didn't know how much of it was true. And you were only a littl'un. What good would have come of it? I didn't want to frighten a little lass."

Cook drained her cup and then poured herself more tea. "Anyway, not long after he left, the lord and lady died in a car crash. They say Christobel was only twelve, poor mite, away at ballet school. She came back just once, when she was eighteen, to close up the house before she went off to dance with the Company."

Clara thought of the ballet shoe they'd found under the

floorboards. Christobel must have left it behind when she'd come to close up the house. She'd only been six years older than Clara was now.

Cook reached across the table and grasped Clara's small hand in her plump one, warm and comforting and a bit rough in places from years of scrubbing pots and pans. "I moved to the village just before Mr. S. returned and set himself up as lord of the manor—only eleven months old, you were. My Burt had just passed away . . ."

"Our grandad," explained Amelia-Ann.

"Babs had moved back in with that littl'un." She nodded at Amelia-Ann and said, "And her Tom, who was an absolute terror. Mr. S. advertised for a housekeeper, and he got me. I needed that job."

"Well, what did he say to you about Christobel?" Clara burst out.

Cook took a long breath and squeezed Clara's hand. "Not much, ducks, except that the cause of death was unexplained. It was mysterious old business. Your uncle told me that Christobel had to keep you secret—something to do with the reputation of the ballet company. Just nonsense, I say."

"But," said Clara, trying to remove her hand from Cook's but failing because Cook clung on, "why'd you go along with Uncle's lie? That Christobel died when I was born?"

Now Cook did release her hand and got up and left the table. There was an extra-loud crash by the sink and then a sniffle. "A condition of the job was my 'discretion.' I think that's what he called it. And that if I gossiped or speculated, he'd sack me. He said it would be easier for you if the past was kept simple, that no child should suffer such uncertainty about their mother's death."

Clara stared at Cook's back in disbelief. She had thought Cook was her friend!

"Oh! I forgot." Cook turned around. "There's been a man in the village asking about you and your uncle. Talked to Mrs. Price, he did, in the shop."

"Nan! Why didn't you say?" cried Amelia-Ann.

"I'm sorry, ducks, what with this, that, and the other, I haven't had a minute to collect my thoughts. Now what did Mrs. Price say his name was? Ah, that's it. Jackson something."

"What on earth does that Jackson Smith want?" said Peter when they were safely on the train to London. Amelia-Ann had taken them to the station on Dapple, all squeezed together in a row. Now it was just the two of them. Stockwell, who didn't like train journeys, was to stay in the care of Luci and Curtis.

"I don't know," Clara said. The train car was empty, and she had her feet up on the opposite seat. She was still smarting from all the secrets Cook had kept from her.

As the train rumbled toward London, they discussed their plan. They would go straight to the Colindale newspaper library and search for any articles they could find about Christobel. After that, they would go and see Granny. She was getting better, Stella had said, and Peter thought they should ask her advice.

"*Stella* says!" said Clara. "Do you believe her? She locked us in the turret, Peter."

They had barely slept the night before, so for the rest of the journey they dozed and chatted and ate the cheese sandwiches Cook had made for them with doorstep-size slices of crusty white bread. They played the minister's cat alphabet game and I spy, and then Peter showed off, claiming he could name every single ballet that Nureyev had ever danced in: "*La Sylphide, Swan Lake, Sleeping Beauty, Giselle . . .*"

A bell rang in Clara's head.

"*Giselle!*" she interrupted. How could she have forgotten? "That postcard you found on the first day, the one from Rome. It must have been written by Christobel! Have you got it with you?"

He did. It was folded into a tiny square so that it would fit in his pocket. "Here," he said. "Sorry it's a bit creased."

Carefully Clara unfolded it. The Colosseum looked very grand, even if half of it was falling down. She turned the postcard over and read the message again.

"'Dancing Giselle tonight. Wish me luck x.'"

So her mother had been on good terms with Uncle. She had liked him. Otherwise, why would she have written him a card?

Clara turned her attention to the postage stamp stuck neatly in the right-hand corner. It was pretty, blue, with white boats on it. In the corner was a date. She peered at it. The numbers were very small. But there was no mistaking it: 1966. Clara stared, confused. That wasn't possible! She, Clara, had been four years old in 1966. And yet Cook had said she had arrived at Braithwaite Manor when she was eleven months old, which would have been 1962. In 1966, her mother was already dead!

Clara put the postcard in her pocket. It seemed that every time she thought she was getting closer to the truth, something else made it more complicated!

Either Christobel was sending postcards from beyond the grave, or this was from someone else.

TWENTY

IF CLARA HAD THOUGHT LEEDS WAS BUSY, SHE WAS almost dumbstruck by London. How to describe the enormity of it when all she had ever known was an eerie quietness reaching for miles and miles, that endless stretch of sky and moor?

The city was teeming. Teeming with people, buildings, traffic, noise. An endless barrage of sights, sounds, smells; a flickering screen of constantly changing images. Everything was here. Everything! Something caught in Clara's throat. A sense of—what? Of promise? Fear? Whatever it was, it felt scary and exciting, dangerous and exhilarating. This was where her mother had come to ballet school all those years ago! Had she been bewildered by the hustle and bustle of it all, far, far away from home for the very first time?

They caught the London Underground at King's Cross because the newspaper library was situated in a suburb called NW9, which meant right on the edge of northwest London. The Northern Line would take them all the way there and then back afterward, across the city to the south and to Kennington, where Peter and his granny lived.

The train was a dark-maroon color, with sliding doors, a rickety wooden floor, and velvety red-and-green checkered seats. Dangling from the ceiling were rows of straps with black light bulb–shaped things hanging from them.

"Look," said Peter, jumping up and catching hold of a light bulb thing in each hand and swinging like a gymnast.

"Is that what they're for?" asked Clara.

"They're for when the train's jam-packed and there are no seats," said Peter, swinging energetically. "People hang on to them so they don't fall over."

At first, the noise and the utter blackness of the subway tunnels terrified Clara. The cars rattled like old bones, and it was so dark outside the windows that she worried the train might fall off the rails. The stations that they passed through—Mornington Crescent, Camden Town, Chalk Farm—were tube-shaped, with curving tiled walls and long, sometimes deserted platforms; it was a relief when, after Hampstead, they burst into daylight and remained aboveground.

∽

The newspaper library in Colindale was in a flat-fronted brick building with elegant slabs of white stone framing the doorway. The stone above the door was engraved with the words THE BRITISH LIBRARY NEWSPAPER LIBRARY and there was a thin strip of grass running between the building and the pavement. "That's where we had our sandwiches when we visited with the school," said Peter. "I made my own 'cause Granny was ill. Everyone else had ham or cheese, but I had jam."

He sounded angry. Did it matter if you had cheese, ham, or jam? Clara wondered. But then Peter added bitterly, "They teased me—said jam was for poor boys."

"It is not!" said Clara hotly, indignant on Peter's behalf.

Inside the library there was a velvet hush, the kind of all-enveloping quiet where you can hear every creak and sniff. They approached the information desk, the soles of Peter's sneakers squeaking noisily on the polished floor.

"Yes?" The man behind the desk looked up. He blinked

in a surprised way. *Probably not used to unaccompanied children*, Clara thought.

"Please, could we look at every copy of the *Guardian* published in, ummm . . ." Peter paused and looked at Clara. She had worked out the calculations on the train.

"October, November, and December 1962," said Clara.

"That's a fair amount of newspapers. Seventy-eight to be accurate. Are you sure you want all those?"

"Yes, please," said Clara.

"I'll fetch you out ten at a time, then," said the clerk. "Wait in the reading room, please."

In the reading room, there were rows of desks topped with easel-type things, tilted wooden frames the size of broadsheet newspapers with little overhead lights attached. Peter and Clara chose a desk near the window and waited for the man to come back.

"Are you sure those are the right dates?" whispered Peter.

"Yes," Clara whispered back. "I was born in January 1962." Peter nodded.

"And I arrived at Braithwaite Manor when I was eleven months. That would've been in December. Christobel must have died just before that. That's why we have to look at the obituaries for October, November, and December."

They sat and waited. It was very quiet, and all the other

readers looked very serious. A man sitting near them glared for no apparent reason. "Can I help you?" Clara asked, ignoring Peter's nudge.

The glaring man glared harder and said "*Shhh*," which made Clara want to laugh and be noisy on purpose, just to annoy him a little more.

"Watch it, we'll get kicked out," whispered Peter, trying not to laugh himself. Clara stared very hard at the desktop and clamped her mouth shut, too. She could sense Peter wiggling his ears. She wiggled hers. She didn't dare look at Peter because if she did, the laughter would explode and then the glaring man would go and get the clerk and they'd be asked to leave.

At last the information-desk man brought out the first ten newspapers and showed them how to mount them on the easel things.

"Are you looking for anything in particular?" he asked.

"The obituaries, please," said Clara.

"Ah . . . opposite the letters page." The man carefully paged through the paper until he found what he was looking for. "There you go."

They took five papers each and worked their way through them. It was easy to get sidetracked because lots of interesting people seemed to have died in 1962, poets and playwrights, actresses and inventors. When they had paged through the first ten papers, the clerk replaced them with ten more. Clara read about actors, authors, and politicians, but no ballerinas.

"What if she's not in here?" whispered Clara when they were on their sixth set of newspapers.

"But she is!" said Peter, hopping up and down in his seat. "Look!"

And there it was. November 15, 1962.

CHRISTOBEL STARLING 1940–1962

Tributes are pouring in for the young ballerina Christobel Starling, who died suddenly at the age of 22 at the Paris Opera on Saturday night. Miss Starling was dancing the role of Odette in Swan Lake *when she collapsed onstage. Tragically, it had promised to be her best performance yet.*

A statement issued by the Paris Gendarmerie says the cause of death is unknown.

"Christobel was a young, talented, and inspiring dancer," said Madame Petrova, company director of the Royal Ballet. "She was full of

promise, recently promoted to the role of soloist and on track to become prima ballerina. Later this season, she was to tour around Europe dancing in Coppélia, Swan Lake, *and* Giselle. *It is a terrible loss for the troupe."*

Starling spent her early years at her family home in Yorkshire before moving to White Lodge, Richmond, to board with the Royal Ballet School. She became an orphan at only twelve years old when her parents, Lord and Lady Starling, died in a car crash in the Swiss Alps.

Last year Starling was rumored to be involved with Soviet dancer Sergei Ivanov. The two met in Paris when Ivanov was touring with the Leningrad Kirov Ballet Troupe, dancing in the corps de ballet and supporting Rudolf Nureyev. However, after Nureyev defected in June 1961, the USSR immediately recalled several dancers, including Ivanov. Starling was reported to have been heartbroken. It is perhaps for this reason that last year she took an extended sabbatical, returning to great acclaim in recent months.

"She danced with great tenderness," said an

*acquaintance, Svetlana Markova, who is widely
expected to take on her roles. "We will miss her
so much."*

*She is survived by an older brother,
Edward Starling.*

Clara got up and walked out of the reading room, past
the information desk, and out of the library. She looked at
her hands. They were trembling.

"Clara, wait!" Peter had followed her. "Are you OK?"

Clara didn't know *how* to explain what she was feeling.
Part of her was reeling with this new piece of knowledge
about her mother and the man named Sergei Ivanov. The
other part was experiencing the unpleasant sensation of
feeling almost invisible. A non-person. Like something
floating in space or cast adrift at sea.

"Peter, there was nothing about me," she said eventually.
"Nothing at all. It's as if I don't even exist."

"Remember Cook said that Christobel had to keep you
quiet because of the snooty ballet company," said Peter.
"Perhaps whoever wrote the obituary either didn't know
about you or was keeping you a secret, too." He laid his hand
gently on her arm, like an anchor, grounding her, giving her
the courage to think the other, bigger thought.

Was Sergei Ivanov her father? And if he was, did he know about her? Could he still be in Russia? Russia was thousands of miles away!

But just as Clara pictured herself embarking on an epic journey, a firework exploded in her head, blasting everything else away.

"Peter!" she yelped. "The poster, in Leeds library, remember?" The fiery reds and yellows, the ballerina with the cat's eyes, the other dancer leaping, in full flight.

She saw the realization spread across Peter's face, his excitement matching her own.

"The Kirov Ballet!" he said. "The same company that Sergei what's his name was with. And they're coming to London!"

"We can find out where they're performing and see if anyone knows anything about him," said Clara.

And then Peter spoke out loud the bigger thought that was ricocheting around Clara's head.

"Clara! This is the best clue yet. This Sergei guy. He might actually be your dad!"

TWENTY-ONE

*T*HEY WENT OVER TO THE NEWSAGENT'S OPPOSITE
the library and bought two Curly Wurly bars, two trian-
gular cartons of orange juice, and a copy of the *London
Evening Standard*. Peter knew exactly where to find the
theater listings at the back.

"Look," he said, stabbing his finger at the page in front
of him.

> *Kirov Ballet returns to the Royal Opera
> House, Covent Garden: Saturday, February 23–
> Saturday, March 2.*

"That's tomorrow!" said Clara, hardly believing their
luck. They could go to the Opera House and find someone

who knew Sergei, who may even have known Christobel. It was all slotting into place.

$\backsim$

As the train clattered back across London, Clara wasn't bothered about the noise or the dark. All she could think about was tomorrow and what might happen. She hugged herself in anticipation. At last, she was going to get some answers to her mysterious past.

Peter, meanwhile, was excited about seeing his granny. "She's going to get the surprise of her life when we turn up!"

At the Oval they got off the train and sailed up the escalator to street level, past rows of posters advertising candies and cigarettes and theater shows. Peter wanted to say hello to Stanley, the stationmaster who had found Stockwell, but he wasn't there.

"He clocked off at four, pal," said the man in the ticket office. "Come back tomorrow; he'd like to see ya."

The station was situated right by a massive road junction, and after the relative quietness of Colindale, the noise hurt Clara's ears. She followed Peter along the traffic-choked road, past the tangle of buses and trucks, cars and taxis, and wondered how they didn't crash into one another. After a short while, they turned onto a quieter side street and then cut across a vast expanse of green that Peter said was Kennington Park.

It was almost dusk. On the far side of the park, six giant tower blocks loomed into the purply-pink sky. In the fading light, they were like beacons, the last glimmers of wintry sun winking and glinting on the hundreds of windows that studded their sides.

"That's our block," said Peter proudly, pointing to the one nearest them. "All the way up there on the nineteenth floor."

Clara gazed up. She had to crane her neck to see to the top. She had never seen anything like them. They looked like alien-fairy towers.

Luckily the elevator was working, because it didn't always, Peter told her, and eighteen flights of stairs were a lot to climb. When they emerged on the nineteenth floor, Peter rang the bell of number sixty-four. There was no answer. "That's odd," he said, retrieving a key from under the doormat and unlocking the door. "We only leave the key here when we're out."

"Granny," he called, running in ahead of Clara. "Granny, I'm home."

Clara followed Peter into the apartment and waited in the living room. It was neatly furnished with a nubby green three-piece suite, a round dining table with two chairs pulled up to it, a small TV, and a gas fire. Above the gas fire was a mantelpiece, on top of which were framed photographs of Peter as a little boy and a small vase filled with dried flowers. It was comfortable and cozy and it was Peter's home. It was easy to picture him here, snuggled up to his granny watching one of their favorite TV programs.

The most impressive thing about the room, though, was the window. It was floor to ceiling and through it you could see the whole of London stretching away as far as the eye could see. There were billions of people out there, thought Clara. Billions and trillions, and they all had their own complicated, tangled lives. She imagined all their hopes and truths, all their secrets and lies twirling and swirling in an invisible mass above the city.

"Clara, she's not here! Where is she?" Peter burst into the room and then out again in a whirl of anxiety.

Clara followed him into his granny's bedroom. Like the living room, it was very neat: not one wrinkle on the lemon-colored bedspread; a silver-backed brush and comb on the vanity; a pot of hand cream scented with lily of the valley; and a book—Agatha Christie's *Murder on the Orient Express*—on the bedside table. Everything was spotlessly clean. The bed didn't look like it had been occupied for a while.

"The Framlinghams!" Peter spun around so quickly he bumped into Clara. "Stella said they were helping take care of her. Remember? Mr. Framlingham is the lawyer who helped her adopt me. She must be staying there!" He smacked his forehead with his hand. "Why didn't I think of that before?"

∿

It was half an hour by bus to Herne Hill, where the Framlinghams lived. Clara and Peter walked back across the park to the road, which seemed even busier than before, the traffic bumper to bumper, crawling along at a snail's pace. It was almost dark, and the streetlamps were on.

"Rush hour," explained Peter. They boarded the number three bus, which was jammed full of commuters on their way home from work. Outside, more people sped along, heads down, coats buttoned up, hands grasping briefcases, newspapers, and umbrellas.

"Move down, move down," the conductor sang. He wore a machine around his neck, and when he turned the little lever at the side, it made a whirring noise and a ticket shot out of the front. There were no empty seats, so Clara and Peter stood squished between the other passengers. As the bus trundled along, stopping and starting, the conductor chatted and sometimes even burst into song. Everyone seemed cheerful despite the crush.

They left the warmth of the bus in Herne Hill. Here the streets were more like avenues, wide and quiet with gargantuan trees erupting from the pavement, bare branches glittering like lacework in the light of the streetlamps. Instead of shops and apartments, there were proper houses with gates and front gardens. The houses had smart front doors and big bay windows. Where the curtains weren't yet drawn, Clara could see pianos, bookcases, a table set for supper.

"Here we are." Peter pushed open a gate to a house that, unlike most of the others, was shrouded in darkness.

He rang the doorbell and waited. Clara blew on her hands. It was cold. She jumped up and down and flapped her arms to keep warm. Peter rang the doorbell again and then bashed the knocker, which was in the shape of a lion's head.

"No one's home," said Clara. Maybe the Framlinghams had taken Granny out for the day.

Peter put his finger on the buzzer and held it there.

Then he lifted the letterbox and shouted through it. "Mrs. Framlingham! Mr. Framlingham! It's Peter!"

"For goodness sake!"

A lady had emerged from the house next door.

"What is this racket? They're not home!" said the

lady angrily. Then her face softened. "Oh, Peter, isn't it? Grandson of Elsa? The cleaning lady?"

"Why aren't they in? Where are they?" demanded Peter. He sounded a bit rude, thought Clara, but she knew it was because he was worried. Where *was* his granny? She felt a tremor of anxiety on his behalf.

"They're on vacation in Malaga. Not due back until next week. Is everything all right?"

"What do you mean, Malaga? They're supposed to be looking after Granny!"

"Is Elsa not at home?" asked the lady, frowning. "Who is looking after you, Peter? Come in, and we'll telephone someone, get them to pick you up."

"No. Doesn't matter," said Peter. He turned abruptly, and this time he didn't just bump into Clara, he actually bashed into her, hard, and ran off down the street, without even stopping to say sorry.

TWENTY-TWO

CLARA RAN AFTER PETER ALL THE WAY TO THE BUS stop. She'd only just caught up with him when the bus arrived and she leaped on, following Peter as he disappeared up the stairs. This time there *were* seats, but it was not a happy journey. All the way back, Peter worried about Granny. If she wasn't at the Framlinghams', where was she? She couldn't have disappeared into thin air.

Clara wished she could do something to make it better. She didn't like seeing Peter's face pinched tight, just as it had been when he first arrived at Braithwaite Manor.

But as they crossed the park toward the apartment building, a sliver of hope crept back into Peter's voice. "She might be back," he said. "She must have been at the shops earlier. The Framlinghams would only go away if she was getting better."

Clara crossed her fingers and hoped he was right.

But when they arrived at the nineteenth floor, they found that the key was still under the mat, and Peter's shoulders drooped. It was then that Clara noticed the door to Apartment 63 was ajar.

"Peter," she whispered, nudging him gently and pointing toward the door.

Peter stopped in his tracks. "That's Stella's apartment!" They heard a bang and a crash. It sounded like every cupboard and drawer was being opened and closed. And then Peter sprang to life and took one, two, three steps across the hall. Was he just going to barge straight in there? Clara clutched him and shook her head.

"She followed us!" whispered Clara.

If they went into Stella's apartment now, she wasn't sure what would happen. She couldn't risk Stella interfering with their plan to go to the Royal Opera House tomorrow.

"But I need to ask her where Granny is!" Peter twisted out of Clara's grip.

Another bang. Footsteps getting closer.

"Not now," said Clara, grabbing Peter again and pulling

him back inside the elevator. She jabbed at the ground-floor button. A long shadow loomed toward them. She jabbed at the button again, once, twice. The shadow lengthened, darkened. *Come on!* And then . . . *swish*. The doors slid to a close just in time.

"Clara, what are you doing?" Peter looked furious. "If that's Stella, I need to have it out with her. She told me that the Framlinghams were looking after Granny, and they're not!"

"Not now. Not yet," said Clara. She didn't want a confrontation with Stella. She couldn't be dragged back to Yorkshire and away from the Kirov Ballet Company. "Get a move on!" she shouted at the elevator. It was so slow, clunking clumsily down.

Upstairs, Stella would be waiting for its return. Or maybe she was already running down the stairs. Clara hadn't forgotten the way she'd run so fast across the moors.

At last the elevator shuddered to a halt and the doors opened. Clara stepped out and waited for Peter to follow her. He regarded her mutinously, and for a second she wondered if he was going to press the button and whizz straight back up. "Please?" she pleaded, and after another few long seconds he nodded and they exited the building together into the cold night air.

It was properly dark now, and the lights of the traffic winked at them from the other side of the park. It was tempting to run, hop on a bus, get lost on purpose. But common sense told Clara it would be better to hide, to wait and see if Stella followed them out. A large bush was growing by the entrance of the apartment building. "Behind there," Clara said.

There wasn't much space, and the twiggy branches snagged their hands and faces, but there was just enough cover if they huddled down low. If Stella came now, Clara thought, she would sail straight past them. Except—what was that? Something was crashing through the under-growth toward them, and it wasn't from the direction of the apartment building. There was a snap and a crack, and then something soft and shaggy flung itself at Peter, and a wet nose nuzzled him and then Clara.

"Buster!" Peter's arms encircled the dog, and it snuffled happily. "Mr. Sealy's dog, number sixty-one, eighteenth floor," explained Peter. "You haven't seen me for a while, have you?" he said to the dog, and they gently headbutted each other.

"Tell it to go!" squealed Clara.

"Just had your walk, Buster?" said Peter. He turned to Clara. "They race the last bit. Buster up the stairs and Mr. Sealy in the elevator."

Clara's heart sank. That was that, then, she thought. Any minute now Stella would emerge, hear all the commotion, and their cover would be blown.

"Shoo!" she whispered at the dog, flapping her arms. But the dog just answered by wagging his tail and gazing at Peter adoringly.

Then several things happened at once. The door to the apartment building slammed open. Someone whistled, and a voice called "Buster!" The dog tore out of the bush; a thud; a yelp; a whimper. And then, "Buster, come here!" And, "Oh dear, sir, you collided with Buster." The sound of someone being helped up, dusted off. Muttered goodbyes. Buster and the man—his owner, Mr. Sealy, Clara guessed—continuing into the apartment building.

Huddled together in the bush, Clara and Peter stared at each other. "It wasn't Stella, then," said Peter. "It was a *sir*."

They crawled out from their hiding place. And there, gleaming white under the streetlamp, was a scattering of small rectangular cards.

Clara picked one up and turned it over.

JACKSON SMITH ESQ.
PRIVATE INVESTIGATOR

Clara shoved the card at Peter as though it had burned her fingers. He'd knocked on the door of Braithwaite Manor. He'd been snooping around in the village. Now he'd followed them here.

"Was *he* in Stella's apartment, then?" Peter asked.

Clara didn't know. Everything was so tangled. He must know Stella. Or perhaps he'd gotten mixed up with the apartments and he thought she and Peter were staying at number sixty-three.

They took the elevator back up and edged silently out; Stella's door was shut and the lights were off. All was quiet. Peter felt under the mat for the key, and they let themselves into number sixty-four.

Peter marched straight into the living room and picked up the phone.

"What's the number for Braithwaite Manor?" he demanded. "I've *got* to talk to Stella now, and ask where Granny is."

"You can't!" pleaded Clara. "She'll want you to go back, and we've got to go to the Royal Opera House tomorrow!"

But Peter was determined. And when Clara told him she didn't know her own telephone number, he dialed something called directory inquiries, and they put him through to Braithwaite Manor. But the phone just rang and rang, and Stella didn't pick up.

In the kitchen, Clara found a tin of soup that she heated up even though Peter said he wasn't hungry. Halfway through the meal, he started crying, and there was nothing she could do or say that would cheer him up. A little bit of Clara was desperate to think about tomorrow, to discuss the ifs and buts and maybes about her mother and Sergei Ivanov. But she had never seen Peter so upset before. She knew she couldn't talk to him about it now, not when he was like this.

~

The next morning, they set off for the train station. They were going to see Stanley. Stanley knew everything that went on in the area, said Peter, and he would know where Granny had gone.

As soon as they walked into the station, a beaming man in a London Underground uniform hurried across to them. "Peeet-errrr, I'm happy to see you back! You goin' to see your granny? I was up at St. Thomas's yesterday, and I told her, 'I'll make you one of my special pineapple rum cakes.' I'll get it now, and you can take it with you. It will bring a smile to her face, for sure."

But for some reason, Peter didn't answer, and when Clara

looked at him, she saw that the color had drained from his face, as if Stanley had said something awful.

"Thanks," said Clara, because she could see that Peter wasn't going to. "I'm Clara," she added, holding out her hand.

"Stanley," he said, shaking Clara's hand warmly. "Any friend of young Peter's is a friend of mine. One minute, I'll get the cake . . ."

Stanley disappeared into the ticket office.

"St. Thomas's?" Peter finally managed. He looked frantic. "Clara, we've got to go there now!"

"What's—?" Clara started. But Stanley was hurrying back from the ticket office bearing a large cake tin stamped with palm trees, and Peter had gone without even saying goodbye.

"She might not be able to manage much of it yet, but she can share it with the nurses—" Stanley stopped midsentence, gazing after Peter's disappearing figure. He turned to Clara, perplexed. "He in a hurry?"

Clara took the cake tin, muttering apologies. Nurses! Now she understood. "He's just worried about his gran," she said, backing out of the station. The cake tin weighed a ton.

No wonder Peter had looked so agitated. His granny wasn't getting better. She was in the hospital.

TWENTY-THREE

*ST. THOMAS'S HOSPITAL WAS UNDERGOING RENOVA-*tions. A brand-new wing was being constructed, and the site was chaotic with scaffolding and cranes. Peter and Clara made their way through the cacophony, following signs to the East Wing, which was quieter and calmer, and then to the information desk.

"We've come to see Mrs. Trimble," said Peter.

"Which ward?" The lady behind the desk pushed her glasses down and looked at them, waiting for an answer.

"Umm, we don't know," said Clara.

"When did she come in, then?"

"Not sure."

The lady sighed. "Well, that's not much help, is it? Hold on, then. Mrs. Trimble, you said?"

The lady rose and started to flick through some cards in a filing cabinet.

"You're in luck," she said, returning to the desk. "She was moved out of intensive care yesterday, where children aren't allowed. But she's in the Willoughby Ward now. Visiting hours are from two till four." She glanced at her watch. "You're a bit early. But go on up, third floor, and follow the signs. Be nice and the nurse might let you in."

It was the first time Clara had set foot in a hospital. She was struck by how quiet it was, a bit like the library, although more antiseptic smelling. They walked along a series of long corridors, passing a cluster of wards named after flowers: Iris Ward, Chrysanthemum Ward, Rose Ward. Mysterious signs pointed off in various directions: Immunology, Hematology, Microbiology. Every now and then, a doctor or nurse walked swiftly past them, purposefully, seriously, thought Clara, probably on their way to save somebody's life.

"Here it is," said Peter. The door to Willoughby Ward was closed. He peered through the glass.

"It's not visiting hours yet." A nurse had appeared behind them. She wore a crisp pale-blue dress trimmed with a white collar and cuffs. A jaunty-looking white cap sat on her head.

"Please, I've come to see my granny—Mrs. Trimble," said Peter. Clara watched him as he clasped his hands and gazed imploringly at the nurse. He looked like Oliver Twist asking for more gruel, thought Clara.

"I'll have to ask Nurse Edith," said the nurse, doing a little grimace as though to say *Rather you than me.* She had a small watch pinned to her apron and an elastic belt that nipped neatly in at her waist.

"For heaven's sake, ask me what, Nurse Bridget?" An older woman had pushed open the door to the ward and surveyed them, one eyebrow raised. "Temperatures need taking! Blood pressures need to be checked! What on earth are you doing out here?" This woman's uniform was a darker blue than Nurse Bridget's, with long sleeves. Her black hair was pulled back, which gave her an air of severity. Yet her eyes were kind, thought Clara.

"Sorry, Nurse Edith! I was just coming," said the younger woman. "I just went to—"

"I know, buy Mrs. Neil some more peppermints," finished Nurse Edith for her. "Nurse, how many times do I have to tell you? Don't let those patients take advantage of you!" She thrust the clipboard she was holding into Nurse Bridget's hands. "Now, do the rounds and report back to me when it's all done. Chop-chop."

"Yes, Nurse Edith." Nurse Bridget looked like she was about to do a sort of salute but then thought better of it and hurried off.

"Now, children." Nurse Edith turned to Peter and Clara. "How can I help?"

"We've come to visit my granny," said Peter. "Elsa Trimble."

Almost imperceptibly, the nurse's eyes widened. "Are you Peter?"

"Yes."

"Well, what's taken you so long? She's been asking for you. Follow me."

Clara and Peter followed Nurse Edith into the ward and past a series of curtains drawn around what Clara guessed must be hospital beds. The nurse stopped just before the last one and turned to them. She looked grave.

"Your granny has been very ill," she said in a low voice, looking carefully at Peter as she spoke, almost as though she were worried her words might make him splinter and break. "But she's going to get better. We can tell she's made of strong stuff. You can see her, but you must be quiet and calm and not upset her. Just ten minutes today, and then you can come back tomorrow. Understood?"

They both nodded emphatically, and Nurse Edith pulled the curtain back a fraction.

"Elsa, dear, look who is here! He's come to say a quick hello before your rest. He'll be back tomorrow." Nurse Edith gestured for Peter and Clara to go in. "I'll be in my office at the bottom of the ward. Pop in to say goodbye before you go."

Elsa Trimble looked very small and pale against the puffed-up pillows of the hospital bed, but her blue eyes sparkled with pleasure when she saw Peter. She didn't look nearly as old, nor as granny-like, as Clara had expected.

"Granny!" Peter was at the bedside in an instant, holding on to Elsa's hand as though he would never let go. He brought his straw-colored head down next to her silvery one and kissed her on the cheek.

"Dear Peter," said Elsa. She had a husky, warm voice. "I've missed you so much! I'm so glad Stella's brought you back. And is this Mr. Starling's niece? Stella said when she arranged the visit that you would have someone to play with."

For a fraction of a second, there was a silence while Peter's eyes met Clara's, and they both understood that now was not the time to tell Elsa they had run away from Braithwaite Manor. Nurse Edith had said not to upset her.

"It's been lovely having Peter." Clara smiled, depositing Stanley's cake on the small table next to the bed.

"How was Yorkshire?"

"Fantastic," said Peter. "Clara's house is enormous, with a turret and everything. And we made friends with some children in the next village. It was fun!"

When Elsa looked at Peter, her gaze was so full of love that Clara felt a pang.

"Is Stella here?" asked Elsa. "I need to thank her for everything she's done. Looking after you all this time! I feel terrible, all the favors she's done for me."

"She's doing some shopping and picking us up afterward," Clara said, because she could see Peter struggling to find the right words. "She said get well soon." Clara smiled at Elsa. "I like your apartment, by the way—it's lovely."

Elsa beamed at Clara, and all of a sudden Clara could see what she would look like when she was well: strong and full of energy—and kind, too.

"I was feeling so much better!" she said. "And I could tell Stella wanted to visit you and Mr. Starling and have a break herself. I said I could manage, and in the end she gave in, left me some soup—all I had to do was heat it up. And then, honestly, the next day I felt so ill, worse than ever before."

"Oh, Granny," said Peter. There were tears in his eyes. "What did you do then?"

"Thank goodness Mrs. Framlingham phoned from Spain, just on the off chance to see how I was! Nurse Edith told me they phoned for an ambulance. Mrs. F. knew something wasn't right."

Elsa closed her eyes and sighed. "Anyway, on the mend now. The doctors say I'm making good progress. And I think they're right, Peter. I honestly feel better than I have for months and months. I can feel the energy starting to come back."

After they'd said goodbye—with much kissing and hugging and promises to come back the next day—Peter and Clara made for Nurse Edith's office as promised. The door was ajar, and they were just about to go in when they heard low voices.

"The results came back yesterday. Apparently traces of poison were found in her blood!"

"No!"

"Yes! Pathology thinks she must have been ingesting small amounts over a long time. It was barely traceable."

"Do the police know?"

"Yes. They're going to come in to talk to her today or tomorrow. Did you see the grandson? Lovely little thing . . . Mind you, don't you think Elsa looks far too young to be a grandmother?"

Clara turned to look at Peter, stricken. But he had already gone, the swinging doors to the ward swooshing shut behind him.

TWENTY-FOUR

"WHERE ARE YOU GOING?" SHOUTED CLARA. Peter was ahead of her, flying down the corridor, and he didn't stop, so Clara had no choice but to follow.

Outside, Peter finally paused by the ambulances and waited for Clara to catch up.

"Poison!" he said. "Who would poison Granny?"

Clara had absolutely no idea.

"Has she got any enemies?" she asked.

"No!" Peter said. "Everyone likes her. It must be a mistake. The doctors must have gotten her mixed up with someone else."

"At least she's getting better now," said Clara (who doubted very much that the doctors had gotten Elsa mixed up with someone else). "She's going to be all right, Peter, which means *you'll* be all right. When she's well, everything will be back to normal."

But despite her reassuring words, Clara felt peculiarly torn. Of course she *wanted* Elsa to be well and for Peter to be happy. But that would also mean he wouldn't need her anymore. He and Granny would be back in their apartment living happily ever after, and she would still be all on her own. The thought was like a black gaping hole, a giant chasm, down which she hardly dared look.

"Yes, you're right," said Peter. He took a big breath, in and out, and gave a shaky laugh. "She's going to be OK, and that's all that matters. So . . . shall we go to the Royal Opera House?"

∽

They caught the number three bus to Charing Cross and made their way through Covent Garden Market to the Opera House. They hurried along, heads down and collars up, just in case Jackson Smith Esq. really was following them.

Cutting through the debris of the market square, Peter kicked a rotten cabbage ahead of him like a ball. The market had closed hours ago, but there were still a few workers around, pushing their empty wheelbarrows. A light rain washed the cobbled streets and the smell of ripe fruit and flowers filled the air.

Any other day, Clara would have been enchanted. But as

they got closer to their destination, the excitement she had felt yesterday at Colindale turned to uncertainty, and her stomach clenched tight. It was perfectly probable that the present-day Kirov dancers hadn't even heard of Sergei Ivanov. Worse, what if they *had* heard of him, but the mere mention of his name made their eyes cloud over and their faces fall? For all she knew, he could be an *Uncle* sort of person.

Uncle had expressly told her that her father didn't even know she existed. Perhaps, she thought as the knot in her stomach tightened a little bit more, he didn't *want* to know of her existence.

At last they rounded the corner onto Bow Street, and there was the Royal Opera House in all its magnificence.

They walked past the main entrance and turned left onto Floral Street. Halfway down they stopped outside a grubby-looking door. It reminded Clara of the back entrance to the Metropole in Leeds. "Stage door," said Peter, pushing it open.

Inside, the air seemed to be damper and chillier than it had been outside. A single electric light bulb illuminated a concrete floor and bare brick walls. Ahead of them, a flight of stone steps disappeared into murky gloom. To the left was a counter. Behind the counter, in an impossibly small space, a cupboard almost, sat a jowly man with a down-turned mouth. His small eyes glittered meanly at them as they approached.

"You can't come in here," he barked. "Be off with ya!"

How could he tell them to bug off if he didn't even know what they wanted?

"Sorry to bother you—" started Clara.

"Don't waste your breath 'cause you *are* bothering me. You're not in the Company, and if you're not in the Company, you're not allowed in here." The man paused to have a long, spluttery cough into his handkerchief. "'Specially not kids."

The knot twisted in Clara's stomach. But she wasn't afraid of him. She'd had years of practice with Uncle glowering at her from his study chair.

"Just because we're children doesn't mean you can boss us around," she said. "We wondered if we can speak to someone in the Kirov Ballet Company. We have a very important question to ask."

"A very important question to ask!" mimicked the man. "No, you can't."

"You can't just say no!" said Peter.

"I can and I will. I'm the stage doorman. The gatekeeper to this place," said the man, puffing out his chest so that he appeared to fill the entire cubbyhole. "When you step through that door, if you're not in the Company, you're the enemy."

"We're not your enemy!" protested Peter. "We only came to ask—"

"They're in rehearsal, and then they've got the matinee and then the evening performance. So no." The man clamped his mouth shut as though that were the end of it.

"Can we at least leave a message?" Clara tried again.

"A message to whom?" The door had swung open, and a man swept across the threshold in a kind of glittering whirl. The cramped, gloomy space lit up and a vibration seemed to fill the air. The new arrival looked extraordinary: catlike with long shaggy hair and a fur coat that touched the floor. He wore huge dark glasses perched above astonishingly hollow cheeks. Now he removed them with a flourish and regarded the children with an intensely dark-eyed stare.

He looked, thought Clara, like a film star.

"Mr. Nureyev!" Peter was staring at the man in unconcealed wonder. Clara noticed he was doing something, a sort of scraping motion that might be a bow.

"Are you Rudolf?" asked Clara. Was *this* Peter's hero? No wonder Peter had gone red, then white, then red again.

"*Mister*, Clara!" hissed Peter.

"Rudolf is fine," said the man graciously. "I'm on my way up to see the Company. Did I hear you say you want to get a message to someone?" He had started to mount the steps

that disappeared into the gloom. Clara knew she had to be quick. Peter still had his mouth open.

"We wondered if anyone knows anything about a dancer named Sergei Ivanov . . ." she began.

Mr. Nureyev stopped. Turned around. Came back down. "Sergei? Of course! He is dancing tonight! My poor tormented protégé."

"He's actually *here*?" Clara couldn't quite believe what she was hearing.

"First time in twelve years they've been allowed out of the mother country. So what is this message?"

Peter had overcome his paralysis and had already taken a scrap of paper and a stubby pencil out of his pocket and was furiously scribbling a note. "OK?" he said to Clara.

She took it, her heart in her mouth, and scanned the words.

> Dear Sergei Ivanov,
>   We have to see you about a VERY VERY urgent matter. We have important information about a child of yours. We will be waiting outside the stage door.
>   Yours sincerely,
>   Clara Starling and Peter Trimble

Clara folded the note and passed it to Rudolf. She could hardly believe she might be so close to solving the mystery about her own life.

"You know, he brings true tragedy to the role," Rudolf said as he tucked the note in his pocket.

"Tragedy?" echoed Clara. The man was mesmerizing. She almost felt as though she were falling, falling into the fathomless depths of his eyes.

"He never got over the death of his girlfriend . . ."

"Christobel?" breathed Clara.

"Ah—you've heard the story. Such promise, such talent, and it all went to utter waste. The rumor . . . Should I share the rumor? Yes, I will, it was a long time ago . . . The rumor in the Company is that she was poisoned . . . "

"Poisoned?" Clara gasped. Peter spun around to look at her, horror etched across his face.

But Rudolf seemed unaware of the impact of his words and was already leaping gracefully up the stairs. "Sergei is dancing this afternoon and this evening," he called back. "I shall give him your note and tell him to meet you here after curtain call, tonight at eleven p.m.!" And in a last dramatic swirl, he was gone.

TWENTY-FIVE

They **WALKED BACK DOWN FLORAL STREET IN A** daze. Clara's head was a gray muddle. It was hard to make sense of what she had just heard. Her mother might have been poisoned. Did that mean she had been murdered? Even Peter, who had come face-to-face with his hero, was deathly quiet as he absorbed it all. "Clara, that's two poisonings we've heard about in one day . . ."

But Clara had jolted to a stop. She was staring at a photographic display splashed across the walls of the Opera House. GREAT BALLERINAS PAST AND PRESENT was the headline.

"Peter, look!" She felt as if an icy hand had grabbed hold of her. A terrific shiver slithered up and down her spine. A familiar face stared back at her from a giant black-and-white photograph. A silver necklace with a snake clasp encircled the subject's throat.

SVETLANA MARKOVA read the caption. PRIMA BALLE-RINA 1962–1972.

"That's not Svetlana Markova!" said Peter.

"It's Stella!" Clara breathed out. She remembered the photograph of Stella and Christobel by the fountain. S & C. Two friends?

"'Svetlana danced many roles, including in *Coppélia*, *Swan Lake*, and *Giselle*,'" read Peter slowly.

Stella? A ballet dancer? Clara remembered the obituary. Svetlana was the "friend" who was tipped to go on the European tour and take on all of Christobel's roles.

The postcard. The one from Rome. It was from her. She'd sent it to Uncle when she was dancing a part that would have been danced by Christobel if she hadn't died.

"Peter," said Clara as the horrific realization dawned on her. "Stella knew Christobel AND your granny. And both of them were poisoned!"

Peter sat down on the curb and slapped his head with his hand. "No one knew why Granny was always so tired! It made me feel so angry and fed up. It's why I got into all that trouble at school!" Peter's face was scrunched up, as if in pain. "Oh, Clara . . . do you think . . . do you actually think Stella has been feeding Granny poison?"

Clara slumped down next to Peter. Had she? And had Stella really poisoned Christobel because she wanted to dance all those roles? She must have been so jealous of her! Everyone had thought she was Christobel's friend. But she couldn't have been. She must have hated her!

Terrible as it was, that made sense. But she still didn't have a clue how that connected to Peter's granny. Why would Stella want Elsa Trimble out of the way?

"We need to find the *evidence*, Clara. The poison!" said Peter frantically. "We've got a spare key to Stella's apartment in the cupboard!" His face started to crumple, and Clara felt a rush of concern. All the spirit seemed to have drained out of him. He looked wan and tired.

"At least your gran's safe now," Clara said firmly, and Peter nodded, although he didn't look very convinced. "Wait here," she said. She had remembered Peter's advice about having a treat after a shock. They happened to be right outside a newsagent's, so she went in and bought a chocolate bar and two fizzy drinks.

But when she pushed the door back open and stepped out onto the street, Peter was no longer sitting on the curb. He was locked in a struggle with a tall, thin, black-coated man. Fear clutched at her. It must be Jackson Smith! He'd caught up with them at last.

"Stop!" she shouted. "Let him go!" The man was pushing Peter against the side of a big black car, opening the door, thrusting him in, then slamming the door shut with a loud *crack*.

Clara dropped the chocolate and the fizzy drinks. They landed with a thud on the pavement. She looked up and down the street. No one was around. "Help!" she shouted. But it was too late—the man was coming for *her* now.

"Get in and shut up," he rasped. A metallic voice, grating, harsh.

"Let me go!" she shouted, twisting herself out of his grasp, kicking at his shins, scratching wherever she could. But his arms were strong and his hand rough as sandpaper as he clamped it over her mouth, stopping her screams.

And then in the distance came the sound of a siren, and sensing hesitation, Clara bit down on his hand, sinking her teeth into the bony flesh. Ugh, it was horrible. But it did the trick. The man swore and let her go, and then she was running, flying down the street and onto the Strand. She ran on and on, her heart in her mouth, until she arrived at an enormous square dominated by a tall column and ornamental fountains. Shakily, she sat down to catch her breath. The square was busy, full of people feeding pigeons. There were hundreds of birds swooping down and hopping around. She was safe for now. The man would never dare to try to grab her here.

Was that man Jackson Smith? Had he *kidnapped* Peter? He had tried to capture her, too! Clara remembered the clawing, bony hands and shuddered. Had Stella sent him to get them? To take them back to Yorkshire and . . . poison them, too? A gaggle of children clambered onto a giant stone lion at the foot of the column. Their joyful cries contrasted sharply with the waves of panic scudding through Clara. If only she could be like that, without a care in the world, free to play. But instead she must unscramble her thoughts and figure out what to do next.

She could go straight to the hospital and tell Granny everything. But the nurse had said Granny mustn't suffer any shocks if she was to get well. She could go to the Royal Opera House and somehow get through to Sergei. But he was dancing all afternoon and evening. And anyway, he might think she was utterly mad.

The only thing left was to go to the police. But first she had to get the evidence, like Peter had said. They had to be able to prove that Stella was a criminal.

∾

Miraculously, Clara managed to find her way back from the square to Whitehall and onto a number three bus. For a minute, relief cut through her anxiety. Thank goodness she had paid attention to their route on the way here. The last thing she needed now was to get lost.

By the time she stepped off the bus in Kennington, a late afternoon fog had descended. She was cold and scared. She was worried there might not even be any poison in the apartment. Surely Stella would have covered her tracks. And meanwhile, Peter might be in the gravest danger.

Thankfully, the key to Peter's apartment was still under the mat. All she had to do was find the key to Stella's, let herself in, and then look for something incriminating.

Yes, she could do that.

But as she entered number sixty-four, the phone was ringing. Clara froze. What if it was Stella saying she had Peter and she would poison him *right now* unless Clara came back? Clara steeled herself and picked the receiver up.

"Clara!" wailed a voice on the line. Clara let out a long breath and sank down on the nubby green sofa. It was Amelia-Ann. She must have found Peter's number in the telephone directory. "I had to call you! You've got to come now!"

"Is it Peter?"

"It's Braithwaite Manor. Oh, Clara, it's been sold!"

"Sold?" Clara's knees trembled. She was glad she was sitting down. "How do you know?"

"Luci, Curtis, and I were playing on the moor, and we rode past it on Dapple. There's a sign outside."

"What sign?"

"It says MORDENS' HOME FOR UNWANTED CHILDREN."

Morden.

Clara remembered the couple who had come to view the house when she and Peter had hidden in the wardrobe. The couple who had said the house was "suitable for their purposes." What had been their exact words? *No distractions, no peering eyes.* She felt a chill spreading deep in her bones.

"And then Nan was in the shop"—Amelia-Ann was still talking—"and there was a woman in there with the most horrible eyes saying the first two children are arriving today! They've got dormitories set up already and everything!"

Clara pressed the phone receiver so hard against her ear it hurt.

The first two children. Her and Peter?

"Amelia-Ann . . ." She felt as though she could barely

talk. And when the words came, they were quick and breathless. "I think they've already got Peter." The bony hand, gripping her arm. That voice, telling her to shut up as he tried to force her into the car. The harsh rasp, metal on metal, like a knife scraping against a cheese grater. She had heard Morden.

"What do you mean? How do they have Peter? Clara? Are you still there?" Amelia-Ann was shrieking over the phone at her now.

"Yes. I'm coming. I'll be there tomorrow. Will you meet me? Promise?"

Clara's heart was hammering as she replaced the receiver on its cradle. Was Stella in league with the Mordens? She raced into the kitchen. There in the cupboard was the key. Clara grabbed it. She slammed out of Peter's apartment, crossed to number sixty-three, and shoved the key in Stella's lock.

Stella's apartment was exactly the same as Peter's but more sparsely furnished and without any of the warmth. Clara crashed from room to room, banging open cupboards, looking under the bed, searching for . . . what? A brown bottle? A green bottle? What color bottle denoted poison? Something with a skull and crossbones on it to warn of dangerous contents? But the kitchen was meticulously clean, the cupboards were practically bare, and there was not a trace of anything, liquid or powder, that looked remotely poisonous. A search of the bathroom and bedroom also yielded nothing.

There was nothing under the sofa or the bed, or in the wardrobe, the chest of drawers, or the cubbyholes that lined the living room walls.

Clara moved to the window and looked out. The view was different on this side of the building. Instead of looking out onto the center of the city, here the crush of buildings began to thin out, and far away in the distance, you could just about make out more space, woods, and fields. "Think, Clara, think," she said, resting her head against the cold glass. What else had Peter told her about Stella?

What had she forgotten?

And then it came, the truth, a thunderbolt, crashing down on her like a heavy weight. The soup! Peter had told her about the soup! The soup that Stella had so "kindly" made for Granny every day. The soup she'd left for her when she'd departed for Braithwaite Manor. The soup that Granny had told them she had consumed before taking a turn for the worse.

Clara hurled herself into the kitchen and wrenched the fridge door open. There it was. An innocent-looking

Tupperware container full of soup. Yet it was far from innocent. It was probably deadly.

Clara yanked open the kitchen drawers. She only needed a sample. Enough for testing. She found a jumble of old plastic film canisters. Quickly, she opened the Tupperware and decanted a small amount of the liquid into one of the canisters. Then she stuffed it into the waistband of her jeans for safekeeping and ran.

TWENTY-SIX

THERE WAS NO TIME TO GO TO THE POLICE—SHE had to get to Yorkshire as soon as possible. It would mean taking the Underground to King's Cross Station, then a train. And then what? A taxi across the moor? She hadn't given a thought to the journey on the way here with Peter. Tackling it on her own was quite a different thing.

She glanced at the star-shaped clock on Peter's living room wall. It was already seven. At this rate, she wouldn't arrive at Braithwaite Manor until past midnight. Abruptly, she gathered her stuff and left the apartment, tearing across the park and along the road until her breath came in great shuddering gasps. By the time she got to the Oval station, she could barely stand straight.

"Clara, isn't it? What's the hurry?"

It was Peter's friend Stanley, looking at her in a funny way.

"Got to get back to Yorkshire," she panted. Peter had trusted Stanley. She would have to as well.

"Where's Peter? With Elsa?" He was still looking at her oddly. And then she realized. It was the way Cook and James used to look at her. It was the look of care. Of proper concern.

"No. He's why I've got to get to Yorkshire."

"Does Elsa know?" Stanley looked serious. For the first time in ages, tears pricked at Clara's eyes.

"No," she said, taking a deep breath. She *would* trust him. "And she mustn't know, not yet. She mustn't worry. The nurse said."

Stanley was quiet for a moment. His eyes had seemed to soften when he had spoken Elsa's name. Now Clara could almost see the thought patterns drifting across his face. "Come on, then," he said at last. "My shift's over. I'll come with you and make sure you get safely on the train."

It was eight stops on the Underground. They sat in the last car, and Stanley chatted to the guard, who was Stanley's friend and who let Clara sit on the special guard's seat.

At King's Cross, they walked briskly to the platform. But when they got there, the gates were shut, and a chalk notice read:

**RAIL SERVICING THIS WEEKEND.
NO TRAINS BETWEEN 7 P.M.
SATURDAY, FEBRUARY 23, AND
7 A.M. MONDAY, FEBRUARY 25.**

"But that's too late!" yelled Clara. People were looking at her, but she didn't care. So what if they thought she was having a tantrum. How could she possibly get to Braithwaite Manor if there were no trains?

Stanley stood clicking his fingers. Was he humming? A sort of thinking hum. He seemed to be considering something.

"Is it very important that you get to Yorkshire? Very, very important?"

"Oh yes!" cried Clara. "Mrs. Trimble would want me to; I know she would!"

And then she saw resolve flash across Stanley's face, and she knew he had made up his mind. "Follow me," he said, still clicking his fingers, and he strode away. So Clara followed, and he led her to a narrow road along the side of the station where a queue of taxis snaked along. She waited while he talked to one of the taxi drivers, who pointed several taxis down, and then the driver of the taxi he was pointing at leaped out and he and Stanley greeted each other like long-lost brothers. Except it turned out they really were brothers (not long-lost ones) and the brother was named Terence, and he clicked his fingers just like Stanley and said, "Sure! No problem! Anything for my brother!"

Terence, Stanley explained to Clara, would drive her all the way. Clara couldn't say thank you enough. No wonder Peter liked Stanley so much.

By the time Clara climbed into the cab and the engine thrummed into throaty life, it was dark. She asked Terence if he could drive via the Royal Opera House, and when they pulled up outside the stage door, Clara went in, determined not to be put off by the doorman.

"Sergei Ivanov is coming down to meet me and my friend after the show," she told the mean-eyed man. "Tell him we're sorry, but *his daughter* has had to go to Braithwaite Manor in Yorkshire, near Leeds." The mean-eyed man stared at her as though he couldn't believe her audacity. "You'd better tell him, or Mr. Nureyev will have something to say about it," she added threateningly. And to her relief, he nodded.

She had done what she could. She still didn't know if Sergei Ivanov *was* her father. But she had left him a clue. What he chose to do next was up to him.

The journey was a long one. They took the highway, and Terence drove so fast the trees and houses and pylons whizzed by in a blur. To pass the time, he told her about the games he and Stanley had played when they were boys in Jamaica, catching crabs and playing in the pumpkin vines; how when they came on the boat to England it was so cold they had to stay inside for a whole week. His words soothed Clara. He was happy for her just to listen and didn't bombard her with questions that she didn't have any answers for.

It was very late when they finally arrived. Clara asked him to drop her a short way from Braithwaite Manor.

It was a black night, a dark night. The wind howled, and icy specks of rain pricked the air. "I'll be fine. I'm going to surprise them," she reassured Terence as she climbed out and waved him off.

She watched as the taillights of the cab got farther and farther away, and when they were just dots in the distance, she turned and ran toward the house. "Peter, I'm coming," she said out loud. She didn't know why, but speaking the words somehow made her feel braver.

The house loomed into view, dark and forbidding as always. And there was a huge sign towering outside, just as Amelia-Ann had described.

MORDENS' HOME
FOR UNWANTED CHILDREN
CHEAP RATES, APPLY WITHIN

Peter was in there, and Clara was going to rescue him. But as Clara ran toward the door, her foot caught on something. She went flying through the air and crashed with an almighty thud to the ground. There was a moment of searing pain, and then everything went dark.

∽

Hours later, Clara woke to find herself in the governess's old bedroom, except that it had been turned into a dormitory with six narrow beds lined up in rows. Her head throbbed and her ribs ached; even the murky morning light, seeping dully through the window, hurt her eyes. She groaned and rolled over, every bone in her body grating painfully against the hard mattress. She felt groggy and listless. For what seemed like a long time, she lay there, stiff as a board, barely able to move.

"Well, well, well, look who we have here, then," came a stone-cold voice. "Nice of you to drop by. I'm very upset you didn't come with Morden when you were meant to."

Clara opened her eyes. A large woman was standing at the foot of her bed. She had the palest blue eyes that Clara had ever seen, hard and flinty like tiny chips of ice.

"You must be Mrs. Morden?" ventured Clara. She would start by being polite, she thought.

"Call me Matron," snapped the woman. "Now you're an inmate. Put these on." She tossed some gray items of clothing at Clara. "And don't forget the cap."

Clara sat up and kicked the clothes onto the floor. Polite wasn't going to work. "You're not having this house," she said boldly.

Matron laughed. It sounded hollow and devoid of any warmth.

"You're too late, little girl. Your brother—"

"He's not—"

"Do NOT interrupt! If there is one thing I cannot abide it is children who speak when they are not spoken to. You'll learn *that* soon enough now that you're here."

The woman paced up and down. She was holding a stick, Clara noticed, which she tapped on the floor at intervals. "As I was saying, the boy and you are our first inmates. You come with the sale of the house, as it were." She gave a thin-lipped smile. Clara did not smile back.

"Where is Peter?" She had been right. He *was* here. "Can I see him?"

"You most emphatically cannot. We keep boys and girls separated."

"Can I go to the bathroom, then?" If she could just get out of the room, maybe she could see a way to escape.

"Use the pot under your bed. Then pick up those clothes and get dressed. I shall come and get you in half an hour." Mrs. Morden tapped her way to the door and then turned back. "Breakfast. I've left some porridge over there." She pointed to a bowl of gray sludge with her stick and looked at Clara as though waiting to be thanked. But Clara kept her mouth shut.

As soon as she had gone, Clara dashed for the door. It was locked.

"Let me out!" she shouted. "You can't lock me in!"

What had they done with Peter? And where was Stella? Was she here, too?

A sob rose in Clara's throat. She felt like she was in a fog—she couldn't think properly. "Peter!" she shouted. "Peter!" she shouted again, frantically pummeling the door. "Matron, Morden! Let me out!"

Nothing. No one even came to tell her to shut up. She crossed the room back to the bed and sat down, her head in her hands. *Think, think.*

A sudden gust of wind broke the silence; an insistent tap of rain started up at the windowpane. Clara looked up. The sky was the color of dark-purply bruises. She let out a long, jagged sigh. She felt almost as desolate as the moor looked.

She had no idea what time it was, but she guessed it was early morning. She wondered when Amelia-Ann and the others would arrive. She hoped it would be soon.

But she couldn't just sit here and wait. She had to do something.

Clara had a sudden flash of Peter trying to stuff his foot into Christobel's ballet shoe, pirouetting across the room, laughing. And then an image of him turning out his pockets to find the flashlight and that glimpse of her red ribbon. When she found him, she would tell him he could keep it.

Clara leaned her head against the windowpane and sighed. It rattled gently. She tugged at the sash, and it gave a little. Despite everything, a smile broke out across her face. The Mordens hadn't thought to check the locks on the windows! They didn't know that half of them were broken. She jerked at the sash again and it creaked open. Now Clara knew what she had to do. She would find Peter, then together they would go to the police and tell them everything, and then they would go to Granny.

Clara pushed the sash all the way up and heaved herself

onto the windowsill. The cold air hit her in the face, rushing headlong into her lungs, making her gasp. It was freezing, at least ten degrees colder than it had been in London. Below her, the scrubby patch that called itself a garden hobbled its way down to the tumbledown stone wall skirting the back of the house. Beyond that, the moors swept away, mile upon mile, battered and windblown.

Clara looked down. She couldn't jump. It was too far.

She looked to her left.

If she inched her way along the ledge and took a step—a very long step—she could reach the next ledge and a window that opened into what had been her bedroom. She could see, even from here, that the window was open a crack. Maybe, just maybe, the door to her room wasn't locked.

Clara placed her hands against the rough brick wall, and very carefully, she sidestepped along. *You shimmied down a rope,* she told herself. *All the way from the top of the turret. So you can do this, Clara, you can.*

When she reached the end of the ledge, she braced her left leg and stretched her right one out until she was almost doing a split, and just when she thought she couldn't stretch any farther, her foot made contact with the next ledge. Carefully, she brought the left leg across to meet the right leg. She shunted along until she was in front of the window, bent down, and pushed it open. It was just wide enough for her to crawl through into the room.

Quickly she crossed to the door and gave a silent whoop when she found it wasn't locked. Out in the corridor, she glanced up and down. She was opposite the bathroom. She remembered when she'd first met Peter, how they'd been a team, helping each other stop the flood.

A flood!

Clara almost hugged herself. It would be the perfect diversion!

Matron had said she would be back in half an hour. She'd have to be quick. Clara scuttled into the bathroom and raced over to the once-leaking pipes. Frantically she started to tear off the thick black duct tape, unwinding it around and around. They'd put loads of the stuff on! When she finally reached the chewing gum, it was rock hard. She yanked open the door of the cabinet above the sink and found the nail scissors. She grabbed them and dug the scissors in deep, stabbing at the chewing gum, easing up layer after layer of it. At last she reached the crack, and water, first a dribble and then a steady stream, gushed out. Quickly Clara shoved the plugs in the bath and sink and turned all the faucets on. There, it was done.

TWENTY-SEVEN

AS QUICKLY AS SHE COULD, CLARA CLIMBED BACK out of the bedroom window, made her way along the ledge, and then slithered through the dormitory window. Immediately, she pulled on the scratchy gray woolen dress over her jeans and shirt. It looked like the sort of thing workhouse children might've worn in Victorian times. She'd just done up the last button when the key turned in the lock.

It was Matron, her milky-blue eyes appraising her, her stick tapping once, twice on the floor. "Good, you're dressed. It's time to come down," she said.

In the study, a feeble fire gasped its last breath in the grate. A man sat at Uncle's desk, all bone and paper-white, liver-spotted skin. He looked like a ghost, something half dead. Standing in front of him was Peter, also dressed like a workhouse child. Relief swamped Clara.

Peter turned as Clara came in, and although she could see telltale tracks of tears, he was standing straight and proud. Their eyes met, and there was something about Peter's look that gave her hope. She stared back, willing him to know that she was ready, too. Ready to fight to the end, fight for him, for Braithwaite Manor, for Granny, for Christobel.

"Good," Mr. Morden's cheese-grater voice intoned. "At last we are all here. Your guardian was none too pleased when she heard how difficult you've been."

"She?" said Clara. "My guardian is not a she. *He* is Edward Starling."

"I think you'll find you are mistaken."

Mr. Morden stood up and came around to the front of the desk like some sort of predatory creature. Peter took a step back.

He leaned down and thrust his face inches from Clara's so that she could see his horrible yellow teeth close up. "You need to get it into that thick skull of yours that Matron and I are skilled in the art of"—there was a pause—"*reforming* young people."

Clara shuddered. His breath stank of blocked drains.

"And your guardian . . ." Matron was speaking now,

tapping her stick on the floor to emphasize her words, "is very keen we reform *you*." *Tap, tap, tap.* "Ms. Stella Jones was particularly clear about that."

"You've made a mistake," Clara protested. "Stella was just looking after Peter while his granny was ill. But she's not his guardian. Or mine!"

"Be quiet!" rapped Matron. "Enough nonsense. Ms. Jones is most definitely your guardian"—*tap*—"and she is selling this house to us." *Tap, tap.*

"She can't sell it," Clara cried wildly. "She has no right!"

"Too late," said Matron with some satisfaction. "It's almost done."

"Stella Jones is a poisoner," shouted Peter. "She won't get away with it, and you won't, either. You can't go around kidnapping people *or* buying houses from criminals."

"Oh, we've done nothing wrong," Mr. Morden said quietly. "Your guardian has all the necessary papers. At this very moment, she is with the lawyer, about to sign this property over to us. Brats included."

"You're lying!"

"I assure you, child, I am not. All I have to do is pick up this phone and tell them we have you both. Then the deal can go ahead, and your guardian can be off to South America. I understand that is her intention."

Clara stared at Peter, and he stared back. They had to find out where Stella was signing these papers and stop her monstrous plan. But before they could do anything or say anything else—

"Ugh!" A large drip of water had landed on Matron's nose. "What's that?" Another one—*drip, drip, drip.* They all looked up. The ceiling was bulging, ballooning. Clara crossed her fingers, held her breath. Matron lifted her stick and prodded the protrusion. It was the wrong thing to do. But it was perfect. The ceiling, already weakened by previous floods, yielded like damp paper, a soggy sponge disintegrating. A hole the size of a golf ball bloomed, and water spouted through.

"Morden, what's happening? Fix it," Matron rapped out. In three long strides, Mr. Morden left the room, and Clara bounded after him, ignoring Matron's cries of "Halt! Come back!" As he disappeared up the stairs, Clara tore along the hallway to James's cupboard. There, hanging on the back of the door and neatly labeled, were all the available keys. Was there one for the bathroom? There was one for the study and bedrooms one, two, three—and yes! Second-floor bathroom.

Grabbing it, Clara raced up the stairs. She could hear Morden sloshing around, the squeak of the tap as he turned it off. Quickly she leaped forward, slammed the door shut, and turned the key in the lock. Then back to her bedroom, quick, quick! The hammer was still there *and* the floorboards she'd prized up to rescue Stockwell. She ran back to the bathroom and began nailing a plank of wood across the door. "See what it's like yourself to be locked up!" she shouted through the keyhole.

When she had finished, Clara ran back downstairs and burst into the study. Matron had Peter in an armlock. He was writhing to and fro to escape her grasp, but her grip was strong and she held on fast.

"Let him go," Clara yelled.

"I will not," uttered Matron, scowling and holding her stick out in front of her as if to ward Clara off. Water continued to stream out of the hole. "Where's Morden? What were you doing up there? I'll teach you to disobey me—"

Clara lunged at Matron. Matron stabbed at her with her stick.

Then an almighty crash came from outside. The sound of hooves on wood, a whinny, children's voices.

Finally, Amelia-Ann was here!

The door to the study flew open and a ball of black fur streaked across the floor, barging past Matron and shooting into Peter's arms. It was Stockwell, purring so vigorously she sounded like a volcano about to erupt.

"Get it away!" Matron cried, backing away from Peter and the cat. And in a glorious rush, Clara remembered crouching in the wardrobe and the Mordens' hasty exit when they had realized there was a cat around. Matron was allergic to cats! Clara had told Amelia-Ann about it long ago, the day they had first met. And she had remembered! Clara felt a surge of pride on behalf of her clever friend.

Grinning, Peter walked deliberately toward Matron, holding Stockwell aloft. Back in the wardrobe, Clara had wished for a whole army of cats to frighten Matron off. Now she hoped one would be enough.

Matron cowered and began to splutter and cough. "Get the cat out of here," she seethed. And then her eyes widened as a ginger-and-white tomcat shot into the room, followed by a tiny gray kitten. Close behind came Curtis and Luci, shouting encouragement. "Go, Marvin, go, Pigeon!" they yelled.

Matron's eyes bulged, and she backed up against the wall. "Vicious children," she wheezed, making a feeble attempt to tap her stick. She staggered sideways. A strange strangled sound gurgled its way out of the shocked O of her mouth, then she sagged at the knees and slithered down the wall.

"Tell us where Stella Jones is," demanded Clara, "or we'll leave you locked in this room with the cats."

"At Jarvis and Jarvis Attorneys in Leeds," croaked Matron.

"Is the enemy secured?" yelled Amelia-Ann. Clara could hear her clip-clopping about on Dapple in the hall.

"Yes!" Clara yelled back. They gathered the cats and backed out of the study, slamming the door shut. Then Clara ran to James's cupboard to get the key, and for extra good measure, they dragged as much furniture as they could to barricade Matron in.

"What about the man?" asked Amelia-Ann. She looked magnificent sitting astride Dapple in her yellow mackintosh with her fiery hair glowing, like a Valkyrie come to the rescue in their hour of doom.

"Locked in," said Clara. She could hear outraged shouts and hammering on the bathroom door. Her heart was pounding. "Can you guard them?" she appealed to Amelia-Ann and the cousins. "We've got to go to Leeds—"

"And then London ..." said Peter.

"Go, go!" said Amelia-Ann. "Nan has called the police. And Tom's coming in the car. If you start for the village, wave him down, and he'll take you to Leeds."

Clara and Peter streaked out of the house, along the drive, and onto the little road that snaked its way across the moors. The wind roared, blasting into Clara's face, pushing and buffeting against her body, but nothing would slow her down. Peter was next to her, his footsteps matching hers. A surge of power shot through her, propelling her forward. Her lungs felt like they were about to explode.

"Look!" Peter grabbed her arm and pointed along the road. They stopped, hearts thudding, and watched the vehicle approach. But it wasn't Tom's car. Clara panted to get her breath back, rubbing a stitch at her side. She bent over and breathed in, willing the pain to disappear. The car stopped a few yards from them and Clara rolled her body back up.

The door of the car opened, and a pair of dazzling creatures flew out. Clara stared and rubbed her eyes. It looked like two exotic birds had crash-landed on the moors. She rubbed her eyes again. Was it magic? And then amid the froth of net and lace, she saw the gleam of satin slippers, exaggerated kohl-rimmed eyes—in a flash, she understood.

The woman who had been driving was wearing a tutu. A glittering tiara was perched on her head.

But it was the other one, the man striding toward Clara, who made her heart stop.

It wasn't his costume that took her breath away— although that was magnificent, like a peacock covered in hundreds of thousands of tiny iridescent feathers, blues and greens and mauves and grays.

It wasn't the silvery mask strung around his neck.

It was his features that struck her, features that were familiarly sharp and pointy; it was the rosiness of his cheeks; it was his blue-black curls. And it was the arm reaching out to her and . . . what was that? A starling tattooed on his wrist.

Clara felt a kind of explosion inside. He had gotten her message! He did care! And he had come!

TWENTY-EIGHT

For a long, long moment, Clara and Sergei Ivanov stared at each other. The wind still wailed, the grass still whipped, the rain still fell in sharp, icy shards; but while the world kept turning, for Clara it was as if time stood still. She was utterly transfixed by this person who gazed back at her with equal intensity. It was a warm gaze, a kind gaze. It was a gaze brimming with so much sadness and longing it made her want to cry. And there was something else, too. Something unfathomable, something unspeakable, something profound.

"I never knew," Sergei was saying. He offered his hand, and Clara grasped it, a ship in stormy seas being pulled to safety. It was a smooth hand, a gentle hand; Clara looked at the tattoo again and then up at him, this man who must be her one true father. Her chest, which had been so, so tight, felt like it was melting.

"Sergei Ivanov!" Peter's face was scarlet from the run. He looked like he was about to faint with excitement and worry, all rolled into one. "This is Clara, Christobel Starling's daughter!"

"Sergei, this is why you dragged me here! She is the true likeness of you!" The woman in the tutu was staring at them in delight, looking first at one, then the other.

"I am Ekaterina Rostov," she continued on, her eyes dancing. She hugged Clara and then Peter. "He asked me to drive him, said it was a matter of life and death. Now that I see you, I know why!"

"How did you know where to find us?" Peter managed, his eyes wide.

"Rudolf gave me the note signed with the name Starling," said Sergei. "And then . . . Clara"—he glanced at her, and Clara felt sure he was looking at her the exact same way that Granny looked at Peter—"left another message to say she was coming here. I had heard of Braithwaite Manor, because it was where . . ." He faltered and his face fell.

"Where Christobel grew up?" Peter finished for him helpfully.

"Yes, and where her brother lives," said Sergei.

He had come! Clara crowed to herself. He had told Ekaterina it was a matter of life and death. Sergei *was* her father and he *was* interested in her existence. Uncle had been wrong.

"We have to go to the lawyers now!" she burst out. "In Leeds. Stella poisoned Peter's granny, and we think she poisoned Christobel, too." She was babbling. Sergei was looking from her to Peter. He didn't understand.

"She's selling the house, and then she's going to South America!" she tried again. "We have to stop her before it's too late!"

Clara waited for Sergei to laugh in disbelief or tell her she was being ridiculous. But he regarded her seriously, and she knew immediately he was going to help.

"Ekaterina, can you drive us?" he asked. "We must do as Clara suggests and go to Leeds at once."

In the car, Clara and Peter told Sergei everything. From start to finish, it all came spilling out: Clara's life with Uncle, her abandonment in the village, Peter's arrival, then Stella's; the ballet shoe, the discovery that Stella and Uncle were somehow connected, their time in London, the poisonings.

"And you really believe Stella poisoned Christobel? And your granny, too?" said Sergei when they had finished.

"She's got another name, too," said Peter. "What was it again, Clara?"

"Svetlana," Clara offered. "She pretended to be Christobel's friend."

"But she was her enemy," added Peter.

"Not . . . Svetlana Markova?" Sergei had gone rigid.

"Yes!" said Peter.

Sergei's face paled. "But Svetlana was Christobel's friend! Her best friend!" His voice trembled.

"Is she Russian?" asked Peter. It was something Clara had been wondering about, too. "She doesn't have an accent."

"No," said Sergei. "Svetlana was her stage name. Her real name was . . . let me think . . . Ah, I remember. It was Sue James!"

Sue James, Stella Jones, Svetlana Markova. It was all so confusing. Clara's head reeled.

"Traitor!" said Ekaterina with feeling from the front. "We will catch her, children, never fear."

As they sped across the moors, Sergei told them how he had met and fallen in love with Christobel Starling, how they had dreamed of a future together, how they couldn't bear to be apart. It was so romantic, thought Clara. She could just picture the young couple wandering along hand in hand by the Seine, gazing out over Paris from the Eiffel Tower.

But then Sergei's face darkened, and he described the days following Nureyev's defection; how the Company was rounded up and forced to leave Paris; how he and Christobel didn't even have time to say goodbye.

"I wrote to her every day," he said, his face drooping. But there was no way of knowing if his letters ever reached her or if she had written to him. And less than two years later, news reached him that she was dead.

Sergei rubbed the tattoo on his wrist with his thumb. "It's a symbol," he said, turning his palm upward so Clara could see, "of my eternal love for your mother. She will always be in my heart."

"I am sure she wrote to you, Sergei," Ekaterina shouted from the front of the car, "but in Russia, after Nureyev defected, they would never have let her letters get through to you."

"I cried a thousand tears," said Sergei, looking at Clara, his eyes deep, dark pools of regret. "They said she died suddenly, and no one knew why. No one, not one person, told me about you."

"Join the club," said Peter. "We've looked in all the

papers, haven't we, Clara? No one said anything about her. Not one peep. She was a secret. Even her uncle didn't tell her anything."

"Or Cook," said Clara with feeling.

"When the authorities finally approved this tour, I knew this was my chance," said Sergei. "I would see Edward, and we could talk about Christobel. But when I telephoned, no one answered, and after that, the line was dead."

"The ballet company is terrible—they like to keep the babies secret," said Ekaterina. "Christobel was young, you had disappeared back to Russia, they would have made her keep the baby quiet . . . You know how they are."

"But," Sergei said, "why would Svetlana—Sue, Stella, whatever she is called—poison your grandmother? What is her . . . what do you call it . . . motive? What is her motive for that?"

"I don't know," said Peter.

"But we're going to find out," said Clara.

TWENTY-NINE

THE ATTORNEYS TURNED OUT TO BE ON A STREET very close to Petruschka, up a rickety staircase above a shop selling secondhand books. They left Ekaterina waiting in the car and bounded up the stairs, taking two at a time. But as Clara reached the door with the names JARVIS AND JARVIS emblazoned on a brass plaque, she paused.

"Open it, then!" said Peter. Clara shook her head and put her finger to her lips. She didn't trust Stella one bit. Maybe it was better if, for the moment, she didn't know Sergei was here. "Will you wait out here?" she whispered to him.

Sergei nodded. Clara took a deep breath, opened the door, and stepped inside. Behind a desk sat a small, rotund man. He blinked at the new arrivals in surprise.

"Children, what are you doing here?" Stella whipped around. Next to her, Uncle was staring at them as if he'd seen a pair of ghosts. He tried to stand, but Stella shot out a hand to stop him, her fingers curling clawlike around his wrist. He sat again, scowling wretchedly. It was a familiar look, as if he wished he were anywhere but here.

"She can't sell it!" Clara burst out, ignoring Stella's question and addressing the startled lawyer. "She's not my guardian. She hasn't got the right. Tell him, Uncle. You can't let her!"

Stella turned around properly now, and the look she gave Clara was so violent it almost threw her off-balance. What had happened to that glamorous, easygoing creature? The one who had let them have the run of the house and do as they pleased? This new Stella stared at Clara with such scorching, burning eyes that she could almost feel the hate radiating from her. A vein throbbed angrily at her temple; a nerve twitched violently under one eye. All traces of the benign Stella had disappeared. How had Clara not seen the real person before?

"I have no idea what she's talking about, Mr. Jarvis," said Stella, recovering her composure. She turned back to the lawyer and tapped her long fingernails impatiently on the desk. "Ignore them. Please continue."

"I *said*, she's not my guardian," said Clara, standing her ground.

"She's a fake," said Peter. "Ask her! She calls herself different names, too! Stella, Svetlana, Sue . . ."

"I take it you are Clara?" ventured the lawyer. She nodded. Wasn't it obvious? "Well, well, my dears, these are wild accusations, indeed." The lawyer pointed at the document in front of him. "It says quite clearly here that Sue James is your legal guardian. Your mother wrote a will in which she specifically stipulated that Ms. James was to look after you until—"

"Shut up," hissed Stella.

"Ms. James! There is no need to be discourteous," protested the lawyer, looking hurt.

"But *he's* my guardian," said Clara, pointing to Uncle, who was looking down at his feet. What was wrong with him? Why wasn't he saying anything?

"Tell her, Eddie," Stella pinched at Uncle's sleeve, "so we can get this finished."

Uncle sighed. "There is no question of us not selling the house," he said, his voice flat. "You will be very well looked after by Mr. and Mrs. Morden in the home."

"No!" shouted Clara. "No!" She watched in horror as Stella picked up a pen, signed her name on the document, and then passed it to Uncle.

"Uncle! Stop!" She needed to know why he was doing this. What possible reason could have driven him to it? "We know what happened to Christobel! Did you hate her that much?"

Uncle laid down his pen and turned to Clara. His expression was just as cold and distant as ever, but behind it lay a glimmer of something else. What was it? Turmoil? *Fear?*

"I hated her all right," he said quietly. "That mother of yours could do no wrong. She was the apple of our mother's and father's eyes. Whereas I . . . they never loved me. They expected me to fail. And then when I got caught up in the gambling game, they wouldn't help me out. I was forced to take the jewels. I *said* I would pay them back, but—"

"Eddie! We haven't got time for a canned family history," hissed Stella. "Sign it. Now."

"No, Sue, I won't." He met Stella's eyes, and Clara saw that at last there was a hint of defiance. "Clara should at least know that I never asked you to do what you did. You agreed to befriend my sister, to get her to accept me, welcome me back into the family fold. Not—"

"Puhh-leease," interrupted Stella. "I did the befriending bit—what torture! I got your name back in the will, didn't I? But those things weren't much help to me, were they?"

"No," said Uncle bitterly. "You wanted more. Far more."

"She wanted Christobel's roles, didn't she?" inter-jected Peter.

"And half the family fortune," said Uncle. He put his head in his hands.

"Well, your conscience didn't seem to trouble you much back then," snapped Stella. "You could've gone to the police. But you didn't, did you? Oh no. You toddled straight back here to claim your beloved Braithwaite Manor."

"For pity's sake, what's going on?" The lawyer looked from Stella to Uncle. "Has there been some sort of foul play that I'm not privy to?"

"No, Mr. Jarvis—" started Stella.

"Yes!" yelled Peter. "They murdered Christobel Starling, and they tried to murder my granny! What did Granny ever do to you?"

"Oh, for goodness sake. The little boy doesn't know what he's talking about," Stella said to the lawyer.

Something inside Clara snapped, and rage took hold of her. "You *did* kill my mother!" she shouted, hurling herself at Stella. A great fury pumped through her veins. "And *you* didn't stop her," she screamed at Uncle, kicking him hard in the shins.

"Get your hands off me." Stella's face twisted with venom. But Clara would not let go. Stella struggled and squirmed, wriggled and writhed, but Clara clung on.

"Now, now," Mr. Jarvis said faintly from the safe place behind his desk. "Fighting won't help. I'm sure if we all sit down quietly we can sort this out."

But in answer, Clara dug her nails deeper into Stella's wrists. Stella raised her knee and rammed it into Clara's leg. Clara spat. Stella scratched. Clara pounded and punched, grabbed and kicked, every blow a small compensation for the hurt and loneliness she'd felt for all those years.

And then everything happened quickly. Uncle stood and tried to make a run for the door. Peter yelled for Sergei, and Sergei burst into the room in a flurry of sequins. Uncle, blindsided by this unexpected vision, staggered back and sank down into his chair.

"You!" Stella spat. She was breathing heavily now, a trapped animal, her lipsticked mouth not perfect anymore, cracked and dry, curling down in a contemptuous sneer.

"It's all your fault!" she erupted, wagging her finger at Uncle. "Running away as soon as you knew *he*"—she jerked her head at Sergei—"was coming on tour. Coward! Leaving me to pick up all the pieces as usual."

"Oh, leave me alone." Uncle had his head in his hands. "Why did I ever get involved with you?"

"You, you, you . . ." Stella could barely get the words out, she was so full of rage. "If it weren't for me, you would *never* have gotten your horrible Braithwaite Manor to yourself. You've never done anything right! You messed it all up right at the start when you lost *him*." She pointed at Peter.

"Don't you mean me?" asked Clara. She was genuinely confused. "He lost *me* in the village."

Stella laughed scornfully. "Haven't you worked it out yet, you idiot?" Clara flinched. "Edward left *him* in his basket at Charing Cross! All he had to do was bring you both back to Braithwaite Manor. But he couldn't even get that right. He went to change *your* nappy, then when he came back, the baby boy was gone! I should have known then that he was useless."

"What?" Clara looked from Uncle to Peter. Peter's eyes were like saucers.

"Do you mean—?" started Sergei.

"Clara!" With all the noise, no one had heard more people clattering up the stairs. Amelia-Ann bounded into the room cradling Stockwell in her arms and behind her was . . . Clara gasped.

"This is Jackson Smith," Amelia-Ann said proudly.

An extremely tall man clutching a briefcase ducked under the doorframe. He smiled apologetically. "Sorry, we're a bit late," he said.

"What have you brought him for?" said Clara. Had Amelia-Ann gone mad?

"It's all right, Clara. He's working for Peter's granny! Tell them, Jackson; tell them what you've found out!"

Stella wrenched herself out of Clara's grasp and elbowed her way past Peter and Amelia-Ann in an attempt to leave the room.

"I suggest you stop right there," said Jackson, coolly blocking her way. "The police are downstairs waiting to talk to both of you."

Stella jolted to a stop, and even though she was motionless, something terrible seemed to emanate from her.

"I have here," Jackson Smith continued, reaching into his briefcase, "a copy of the very same document you have there, Mr. Jarvis, and if we read it correctly, we will see that this matter can be settled once and for all. But first . . ." He stepped forward and clasped Sergei's hand in his. "Sergei Ivanov? I am very pleased to meet you. And I see you have already made the acquaintance of the twins."

THIRTY

TWINS! PETER STARED AT CLARA, AND SHE STARED back, and for a minute all the drama in the room just fell away. Then Clara felt the strangest thing. It was as if something unspoken passed between them.

"*That's* why," Peter said softly, stepping close to her so only she could hear. "I felt something here"—he raised his fist and thumped it hard against his chest—"when Morden took me. It hurt. I thought I was having a heart attack! And then when I saw you again, it didn't hurt anymore." And then he was grinning, and Clara was grinning and tears pricked at her eyes, happy tears, and everything felt real and true, and the room shot back into focus, brighter and better than ever before.

"This will," Jackson Smith was saying, "states quite clearly that Sue James is to be the guardian of Peter and Clara *until* such time as Sergei Ivanov, their father, is found." He looked squarely at Stella. "Ms. James, I should also tell you that our police, in partnership with the French police, are currently looking into accusations that you poisoned Ms. Starling *and* used that same poison on Elsa Trimble."

Stella blanched. "It's all lies!" she spat. "You've made it up! You haven't got any proof."

Clara stepped forward. "We do, actually," she said. And a wave of victory swept through her as she reached under the horrible gray scratchy dress to retrieve the film canister of soup that was still tucked into the waistband of her jeans.

∾

It was in a state of high excitement that everyone piled into Ekaterina's and Jackson Smith's cars and drove to London.

Sergei, who everyone agreed looked like the spitting image of Clara, couldn't believe he hadn't noticed that Peter's hair was the exact same color as Christobel's. He had photos in his wallet that he pulled out to show them. Christobel laughing, Christobel jumping in the air, Christobel blowing a kiss to the camera, her curls blowing in the wind, her eyes squinting against the sun. The photographs were faded and worn, but they were infused with a special warmth.

However, while the others all chattered and laughed, Clara found she was almost stunned into silence. Her life had exploded into glorious technicolor. Everything felt enhanced, heightened, as though a painter had taken a brush and boldly swept it across her entire being, banishing all the darkness and making it vivid and bright.

"That's why we can both wiggle our ears, Clara!" Peter crowed. "I should've guessed! Specially 'cause 99.9999 percent of people in the world can't do it."

Clara hugged herself. She felt like she wanted to cry, even though she had never been so full of sheer, utter joy. She was actually someone. Someone with meaning. Not an unwanted niece saddled with a guardian who didn't care for her or even like her. She was a daughter, a *wanted* daughter, and a sister. She mattered.

Her father and brother mattered.

∽

At the hospital, Granny was up and sitting cross-legged on the bed. She looked different, thought Clara. Maybe it was the emerald-green sweater she was wearing, or the plum-colored lipstick, or the gray eye shadow that seemed to turn her blue eyes violet. "No more poison in me!" She laughed and held out her arms, inviting Peter and Clara to climb on the bed. "Children, I want you to tell me everything. From start to finish and not leave one bit out."

"Can I do it?" asked Amelia-Ann. "Jackson told me everything on the way to Leeds. Pretend I'm a lawyer in court laying out the whole dastardly thing. I promise I'll tell it good!"

So Amelia-Ann took the floor, pacing up and down the ward in her white high-heeled shoes and yellow mackintosh, her red hair billowing about her like a crown.

Clara noticed how Peter flopped against his granny. Very gently, she allowed herself to lean against Granny, too. She smelled like sweet orange blossom. One of the nurses went around the ward propping up the other patients against their pillows so they could have a good view of the proceedings, too. Stockwell crept under Granny's sheets and turned around three times before settling.

Amelia-Ann looked very commanding, thought Clara. She could just picture her in the future, holding absolute sway in court.

"Now, Peter," said Amelia-Ann, "as you know, your granny adopted you after you were found at Charing Cross with nothing more than a scrap of red ribbon tied to your basket and your name sewn onto your blanket."

"No!" interrupted Clara. "I didn't know that! What scrap of red ribbon? I thought you'd stolen mine!"

"What do you take me for?" asked Peter. "I'm not a kleptomaniac."

So they both had red ribbons, thought Clara, given to them by their mother. If only they had worked that out before!

"Anyway," resumed Amelia-Ann, "where was I? Oh yes, about a year ago, Mrs. Trimble here . . ."

"Oh, do call me Elsa," said Granny.

"Thank you, Elsa. About a year ago, Elsa asked Mr. Jackson Smith Esquire, the private investigator, if he would look into Peter's beginnings. She thought that one day Peter would want to know more about who he was and where he came from."

Peter jumped off the bed and stared indignantly from Granny to Jackson. "Why didn't you tell me what you were doing?" he exclaimed. Clara couldn't help but silently agree. It would have saved a lot of trouble.

"We didn't want to get your hopes up, in case nothing came of it," said Granny.

"And at that point," added Jackson, "we had no idea your next-door neighbor was involved or how much danger you would all be in."

"You can say that again," said Peter.

"Will you all stop interrupting?" said an annoyed

Amelia-Ann. "I've barely started! Anyway, Jackson went to Paris, where he did some investigating and met the nurse who looked after you two when you were babies. Next, he paid a visit to Stella's apartment and found—"

"We were there!" burst out Clara. "But we hid outside the apartment!"

"Yes, Clara," said Amelia-Ann. "Well, while you were hiding, Jackson found a fake ID. As we all now know, Stella's real name is Sue James. But even better than that, he discovered the twins' birth certificates. Jackson, show them to Elsa."

"Oh my goodness!" said Granny as she scanned it. "Peter, we had to guess your birth date when we found you. So no more birthdays in April for you! It'll be the eleventh of January from now on, just like your sister." The word *sister* gave Clara a warm glow.

"And the other document you found?" continued Amelia-Ann. "The one the nurse said she saw Christobel give to Stella for safekeeping?"

"Ah yes," said Jackson. "That was the copy of the will that Stella was flummoxing Mr. Jarvis with earlier today. She really was charged with being the children's guardian, you know."

"She tricked us all," said Peter. "Christobel, me, Granny, Clara. Even Mr. Starling in a way."

"She could be extremely charismatic," said Jackson. "Many notorious criminals are."

"Clara?" Amelia-Ann said. "D'you want to read this out?

"'In the event of my death,'" read Clara, "'I wish Sue James to look after Peter and Clara. My brother, Edward, shall be temporary guardian of Braithwaite Manor. This arrangement should last until my beloved Sergei Ivanov is able to return. The house shall then pass to him and my darling children. Signed: Christobel Starling.'"

"But Stella didn't look after us!" cried Peter. "She dumped us on him! All she cared about was dancing Christobel's roles!"

"Correct," said Jackson Smith. "And, because Edward was weak and obsessed with regaining control of Braithwaite Manor, he complied."

"But," said Amelia-Ann, "as we heard earlier, Mr. Starling made a mistake almost as soon as he reached England. He lost Peter."

"And just like that, we were separated," said Clara.

"But even so, they thought they had pulled it off. Until—"

"They found out that Sergei was coming on tour!" interrupted Clara, dancing ahead of the story.

"Yes," agreed Amelia-Ann. "Stella knew that if Sergei found out about the twins, he would be entitled to the house. So she planned to track Peter down, make sure that both of you were well and truly out of the picture, sell the house and its valuables, and escape with the proceeds before anyone found out the truth."

"So Uncle wasn't selling all that stuff to pay off his debts?" asked Clara.

"We believe," said Jackson, "that Stella had instructed him to sell as many valuables as he could to fund their . . . retirement, shall we call it? In South America."

"So you're telling us that when Stella moved in last year, she already had everything planned?" asked Elsa. "It's shocking!"

"Indeed, she did," pronounced Amelia-Ann. "She had gotten wind of your investigations, and she knew she had to get you out of the way, too!"

"Hence the soup," said Jackson.

"She knew exactly what she was going to do," added Amelia-Ann. "Poison Elsa, pack Peter off to Braithwaite Manor. The Mordens were offered the house at a good price as long as Peter and Clara were 'included.' The only wrench in the works was your uncle," she said to Clara, "running off because he got scared."

Amelia-Ann had stopped pacing now and stood quietly while everyone digested the dreadful facts.

"Yesterday, I had no children. This morning, I had one. Now I have two!" Sergei exclaimed, as if he could hardly believe it.

"And my *real* name is Peter Starling!" said Peter. "A proper ballet name! Sergei, did I tell you, I really, really like ballet? D'you think it's in my genes?"

"And he's good at it!" added Clara.

She looked at everyone crowded around the bed. Her brother, her father, her best friend. If Elsa was Peter's adopted granny, could she be her granny, too? Clara thought she probably could. She felt a kind of swell, an unfurling of her chest, as if her heart were actually lifting and opening. It was a feeling she had never experienced before, and yet she knew exactly what it was. She felt like she belonged.

TWO YEARS LATER

Newspaper clipping from 1976:

It was reported that yesterday at 8 a.m. GMT, Sergei Ivanov defected from the USSR. The critically acclaimed dancer is currently at an undisclosed location in London. The dancer, who will be debriefed by Her Majesty's Government today, is expected to join his children, fraternal twins Peter and Clara Starling-Ivanov, shortly. The children live with their adoptive grandmother, Elsa Trimble, and her friend Stanley Lawrence at Braithwaite Manor B&B in West Yorkshire. The establishment advertises itself as "a cozy getaway on the wild and wind-swept moors."

Mr. Ivanov's life has been complicated by tragedy. Unable to leave the USSR for many years, news of his partner Christobel Starling's pregnancy and the birth of their children did not reach him and was kept out of the public domain. Her death in 1962 remained unexplained for many years, and it was not until recently that the mystery was finally solved. In March 1974, her colleague Sue James (widely known by her stage name, Svetlana Markova) was charged with her murder, and Ms. Starling's brother, Edward Starling, with conspiracy to pervert the course of justice.

Mr. Ivanov, now 36, is expected to take up a role as choreographer at the Royal Ballet Company. "He is thrilled to be back," said a spokesperson. "He cannot wait to be reunited with his dear children. However, we do ask you to respect his family's privacy at this time."

ACKNOWLEDGMENTS

To become a writer you need to be a reader, so my biggest thanks are to my parents, Moira and Selwyn—both librarians—who throughout my childhood gave me the time and space to wallow in books. To my writer friends: once upon a time, the thought of joining a writers' group filled me with horror. Now I can't understand why I waited so long! Thank you, Heather, Tim, Lis, and Graham. Without our meetings and your brilliant feedback, this book would not have come this far. Thank you, Poppy, Rose, Clare, Pip, Margot, Moira, Lucy, and Henrietta for being my first readers. Your encouraging words really spurred me on.

A trillion thank-yous to my agent, Tessa David at PFD, for scooping me up and believing in me; and to my wonderful editors, Alice Swan and Stella Paskins, for helping to make this story the very best it could be. Thanks to the lovely copyeditor, Maurice Lyon, and everyone at Faber who has worked so hard to bring this book into the world: Natasha Brown, Sarah Lough, Hannah Love, and Margaret Hope. Huge thanks to my US editor, Susan Van Metre, whose enthusiasm for the story blew me away; and to Jo Rioux for her glorious illustrations and Maya Tatsukawa for designing such a wonderfully atmospheric cover.

To Nick (who, like Peter, is a dab hand at cracking a hard-boiled egg on his forehead), thank you for all the cups of tea and always being there for me!

And last, but very much *not* least, thank you, Reader, for choosing this book. *The Secret Starling* will be a tiny piece in the rich patchwork of books you will go on to read. I wish you all the best on your reading journey!

ABOUT THE AUTHOR & ILLUSTRATOR

JUDITH EAGLE has worked as a stylist, fashion editor, and features writer. She currently works in a secondary school library and lives in South London with her family and Stockwell the cat. This is her first book.

JO RIOUX is an author and illustrator who studied illustration at Sheridan College in Canada. She has illustrated young adult novels, chapter books, picture books, and graphic novels, including *Cat's Cradle: The Golden Twine*, which won a Joe Shuster Dragon Award for best comic for kids, and *The Daughters of Ys* by M. T. Anderson. She lives in Ottawa.